The " Runnymede " Series

THE REBELLION OF RITA

First Edition January 1937

HER HEART GAVE A JUMP

THE
REBELLION OF RITA

BY
BERTHA LEONARD

JUVENILE PRODUCTIONS LTD.
LONDON

THE "RUNNYMEDE" SERIES

Twelve handsome volumes for Boys and Girls
uniform in size and price with this volume.

CONTENTS

THE REBELLION OF RITA

CHAPTER I

THE RULER OF THE ROOST

"COCK-A-DOODLE-DO!" crowed Rita's brother aggravatingly.

The acknowledged "ruler of the roost" among the youthful element at Priory Farm, tossed her tawny head imperiously, the golden-brown eyes that so nearly matched it, sparkling maliciously as she made retort to the teaser.

"Oh, your turn will come too, my boy, for there are designs on your freedom, and then you'll shout as loudly as *I'm* doing. School! Ugh! I *won't* go! I simply *won't!*"

The applause of the two younger Conway girls, Poppy and Tessa, was sympathetic enough, but rather lacking in conviction, all the same.

"If *only* you can hold out about it," was the would-be hopeful remark of the former, presently, "but it all sounded so *frightfully* settled."

"Then I'll unsettle it," snapped the rebel.

7

"Oh, but Rita, I don't know *how* you'll manage it," Tessa lamented. "You know what Daddy is like when he's really firm about a thing; one might as well try to push an elephant over as move him from a decision."

"I won't go to school, I tell you; I *won't!*" was Rita's impatient reiteration.

Tessa rambled on gloomily. "Well, then, you'll either have to run away or be ill. I don't see any other way out of it. And if you're not *really* ill, Doctor will find you out in no time, and if you run away, I expect detectives will soon track you down."

"So there you are, Carrots," drawled the boy of the family. "I advise you to give in gracefully and go to school like a good girl."

Rita hunched a scornful shoulder. Although fully aware that his chaff covered real concern over unwelcome news, and a desire to avoid harrowing scenes in the home circle, she had no intention of being influenced by her junior of a year. So, ignoring him, she prepared to interrogate her sisters afresh.

The Conway quartette had foregathered for the "barn" tea that had become more or less an institution on those Saturdays that were hardly genial enough as regards weather, for outdoor picnics. But interest in the refreshments had been temporarily suspended by the shock of the news brought by the twins, who had been despatched by their seniors to fetch the tea, and who, while awaiting their mother in the kitchen in the absence of the two maids, had been eavesdroppers at the service hatch into the dining-room.

"Do you think that that Howard creature actually called in to angle for a pupil for her school?" Rita inquired of the newsmongers.

They looked questioningly at each other, then shook their heads, and Poppy made answer, obviously anxious to make the best of things so far as was possible.

"I don't think so; she seemed to have just popped in as she has done lots of times since she got so friendly with Mummy and Daddy. They were in the dining-room talking over cups of tea, and Mummy was telling her that the drawing-room re-decorating would soon be finished and she wanted Miss Howard to come in for a proper tea party there before her holiday

9

was over. That started Daddy on asking her about the school she teaches in—what it is like and how much the fees are."

"Of course, she *may* have been just waiting for her chance," Tessa admitted, taking up the tale as her co-eavesdropper paused. "Anyhow, she jumped at it. She could *strongly* recommend Camberside to any parents, she said, for both education *and* discipline; she wished she could persuade Mummy and Daddy to try it for you. It would be jolly for you now to be meeting other girls of your own age; the competition and team spirit would be so good for you; you'd be moulded and controlled. As they were finding governesses such a problem for you now, why not give school a trial? Oh, my goodness! She did rattle on in that wheedling voice of hers!" Tessa finished up, with a wry grimace.

Rita's face was granite-like in its hardness.

"The snake! The absolute *snake!*" she ground out viciously. "I should have jumped clean through the hatch at her if I'd been there to hear her. But you said she has gone now, didn't you?"

The twins flashed another lightning glance at each other and nodded hastily, visions of a ferocious fourteen-year-old attacking Miss Howard tooth and nail, floating terrifyingly before them.

Rita snorted again. "Humph! After having got Mummy and Daddy nicely into her pupil-catching net! Didn't *Mummy* make any sort of stand against my being sent away?"

All three of the younger Conways understood the hurt prompting that last question. Rita was the firstborn of the family. In spite of her tempestuous nature and the wildness that characterized the whole brood, Rita was always depended upon by her mother to see that adventurousness stopped short of foolhardiness, and Rita's interest in, and powers of quite clear-headed reasoning upon, matters pertaining to the farm life she loved, had led both her parents to turn very attentive ears to her upon occasion. Even the several sorely tried governesses who had succeeded each other at the farm, had allowed that there was plenty of good in Rita; only it needed directing, and her strong temper disciplining. None of them had come anywhere near accomplishing either, however, and therein lay the snag, for neither Mr. nor Mrs. Conway, with the manifold duties of a very large farm upon their shoulders, had time for the strict supervision they would have liked to give to their children, and which they had so far hoped for in vain from the governesses. The latter, in justice to them it must be admitted, had all found it very hard going at Priory Farm, in spite of the generous salary, liberal board and the freedom of life on a big farm several miles from the cramping conditions of a town.

It was this very distance from anything in the shape of a good school which had kept the Conway children so long under home tuition, and as it had seemed the easiest way out of the educational question for a time, things had drifted on with periodical breezes and changes of governesses, until the arrival of an Easter holiday boarder at one of the farm cottages. In the Conway parents, Miss Howard, English mistress in a big boarding school, found congenial society. To their children she was anathema, because she was a representative of the teaching profession they hated with all their sport-loving hearts. They simply had no use for any purveyors of knowledge, other than those who dealt with outdoor pursuits.

So the stormy eyes that Rita bent on her little sisters were inquisitorial in their searching.

"Don't pretend that things are better than they are," she went on, as with puckered brows they sat on a bale of straw, wondering how best to frame a reply that would not further inflame her anger. "Tell me straight out. Did Mummy put up any sort of fight against the school idea for me?"

The twins squirmed uneasily under the determined questioning. "Not a—a *fight*, exactly," Tessa got out unwillingly. "She said she was afraid you would miss the free life here very much at first and——"

"Of course I should! All the time, too, not merely at first. Well, what did Daddy say to that?"

Poppy chimed in again. "Oh, that you would be coming back to it again. School wouldn't last for ever—only three or four years."

"Years!" screeched Rita. "Why, I should

13

go quite mad before the first term was up, which would mean that I should *never* come back, because I should have to be put in a looney asylum. And all because of that wretched Howard woman coming scratching round for pupils!" and for the next minute or so Rita made what Jimmy called "poisonous remarks" about the teaching profession in general and Miss Howard in particular.

When her tirade came to a temporary end through sheer lack of breath, Tessa asked tentatively: "What are you going to *do*, Rita? You mustn't *know* anything till Mummy and Daddy speak about it, or you'll give Poppy and me away. We oughtn't to have been listening, of course. Mummy and Daddy would be frightfully cross if they knew. It's mean to listen to people; you've told us so yourself, often."

"Only we j-just c-couldn't help it this time, Rita," put in Poppy with the stammer that usually assailed her in moments of agitation. "Wh-what *are* you going to d-do?"

Jimmy hastily heaved himself up from a nest among hay trusses, gripped a flask and spoke firmly as he proceeded to arrange four mugs.

14

"She's going to have tea. We're *all* going to have tea, and not be silly asses enough to let it get cold. After all, we can talk things over while we tuck in, and a lot more comfortably too. Now, calm down, you three, and grab what you want, or else I'll eat *everything*."

Which was Jimmy's sensible and successful way of averting disaster to the twins, by giving his elder sister's temper time to cool.

But the end of the barn tea brought no solution of the much-talked of quandary. Nobody could think of any plea that would be likely to alter the decision regarding Rita.

Not that the Conways gave in without a big struggle for the endangered liberty of one of their number. No! that wasn't their way. So many and sometimes fearsome were the schemes they devised, thrashed out and at length, all being either gloomily or with levity discarded as out of the question.

"There's one way of our all getting out of lessons for ever and ever," Tessa said after one of the universal ponderings. "If only we could manage it," she added, in the tone that invited questioning.

"Well! push on! what is it?" queried her brother impatiently.

"Walnuts, to begin with," she murmured, so dreamily that long stares at her were succeeded by shouts of laughter.

"Poor dear! the shock of all this has gone to her brain," was Rita's comment when she had sobered down again.

But Tessa was not to be stopped by ridicule from airing an idea.

"Or that potash stuff might do; it stains floors, so I expect it would stain skins," she went on.

Rita put a languid hand to her forehead. "Does light dawn on me?" she queried sardonically. "Are you suggesting that we should become a nigger troupe, child?"

"Oh, no!" Tessa sounded scandalized. "I shouldn't like a *quite* black skin; one couldn't be sure it was clean, and I like to be clean sometimes. No, I meant just gipsies, they're nicely brown. The ones who camped here last night were really attractive, I thought, and I don't suppose they have got far, as they only moved on about midday."

"Jimini! listen to her!" cried the Conway son and heir. "We're to dye our little skins and trot after that lot of light-fingered rascals, hey? Why!" here he glared ferociously at Tessa, "what do you suppose they would make us do for our keep? Sneak things out of shops, creep round back doors and steal! Go out poaching at night! First we'd be in prison on bread and water; then we'd end up by being shot by a gamekeeper or somebody. What a life! What a death! No more lessons for ever and ever. Oh, no! Talk *sense*, kid!"

Tessa looked rather aggrieved. "You *would* think of all the awful things, Jimmy," she retorted. "There are plenty of ups as well as downs, in a gipsy life. Anyone would think to hear you talk, that they all died off like flies, quite young, too. But they all look as healthy as anything, and there are plenty of old ones, so there isn't much shooting of them, evidently."

"H'm! well! we won't be gipsies for keeps, anyhow," settled Jimmy. "All right in summer, perhaps, but too jolly cold in winter. Think again, little dotty one."

Accustomed to brotherly criticism, Tessa took the final rebuff good-temperedly, chewing a straw reflectively as she cudgelled her brains for a more acceptable notion.

It was her twin who next broke the brooding silence.

"There's an awfully good dodge some people have for getting their own way about things. What about our all doing a hunger strike?"

"Count *me* out!" was Jimmy's hasty and very decided vote. "What good would having our own way be to us if we all died of starvation?"

"Oh, I didn't mean *that*," expostulated Poppy. "We wouldn't *really* be hungry; we could eat in secret. Lay in a store of food somewhere, you know."

"Oh, no need for that; we'd just bury a few bones and dig 'em up as required like the dogs do. And can't you see us sharing the pigeon's peas and rading the pig tubs?" Jimmy positively guffawed, even the stormy-faced Rita being betrayed into a smile.

But her simmering anger soon blotted it out.

18

"It's all very well to sit here and talk a lot of nonsense," she broke in, spiteful with herself for having been even momentarily diverted; "but we've got to be really serious with my freedom and the jollity of all of us at stake. You others are quite on the wrong track, too. Why should we suffer all sorts of wretched inconvenience fighting for our rights? Oh, dear! if only we could get the whole matter dropped by making the Howard woman vanish!"

"And how?" drawled Jimmy, adding: "If we were conjurers now, we *might* manage it. Bunnies out of hats, bunnies gone again, eh, what?" and he gestured dramatically. "Then there's the black magic of long ago. Pity we don't know enough about that to turn her into an animal and drive her away. I can't think of any other way of disposing of her."

"I'd like to drown her," Rita interpolated viciously. "We could pull aside the old well cover, entice her that way and let her fall down into it. She'd vanish then all right."

Consternation was written large on the faces of the twins.

"Oh! but then she'd haunt us! Fancy if we had a ghost at the farm!" cried Tessa gaspingly.

"Wringing her hands and wailing and trailing her wet clothes all around. Ugh!" was Poppy's shuddery imagining.

"We shouldn't see her for long, because we'd all be hanged for murder. Still! there could be no more talk of school for us then," Jimmy said with a kind of solemn relish.

"No! but things might be lots more awful," Tessa argued strongly. "Perhaps *our* spirits wouldn't rest, either, if we came to a bad end like that. I should hate to think of our ghosts running round the house for evermore, meeting Miss Howard's at every corner. We should *never* see the last of her then."

"So *you'd* better think again, too, Rita," Poppy said, nodding her head portentously, and after that a more level-headed discussion was waged, though all to no purpose.

"No! the break-up of our little band is at hand; there's no doubt about that," was Jimmy's lugubrious prophecy towards the conclusion of the long pow-wow. "I can see myself being cleared out next. You two," this to the twins, "will probably be safe here till Rita and I have finished; all four of us at once at boarding school would be too much for Dad's pocket, I expect."

"It'll be horrid," wailed Poppy. "A governess will simply be able to *sit* on us without Rita and you here to keep her in order."

"Nothing will be a bit the same," came in a groan from Tessa.

"I bet it won't!" This with grimmest satire from Rita, who added immediately, however, "*If* we go! But it hasn't happened yet. Now, you others, get on with whatever you want to while I stroll indoors with the tea crocks. I can't settle to games till I've run across Mummy. If she says anything, I want to air an idea that has just occurred to me and let it sink in before Daddy gets in to supper."

"A *good* idea?" the twins called in chorus after her.

"Grand!" was the laconic answer she flung at them over her shoulder. "I shall offer to *work* on the farm, in the dairy or even in the fields, farm labouring, you know. *Anything* would be better than school," and she disappeared through the barn doorway, leaving her juniors to compare a life that included tennis, driving and horse-riding glories *ad lib*, with one of butter-making, hard scrubbing and so on, or the back-aching job of field planting, hoeing and the like.

As chance had it, however, Rita's first encounter was with her father. Skirting the farm-yard, she chose the shortest route to the house from her direction, and was crossing the stable yard when he emerged from one of the horse boxes.

"Hullo! hullo!" he called out, stopping short and eyeing his firstborn with amused surprise. "Have the worms turned at last, then?"

"*Worms*, Daddy?" Rita had a hard job to make her voice sound quite natural as she halted in front of him.

He looked whimsically down, just an older and a bigger edition of the teasing Jimmy, she thought, eyeing his jolly face searchingly. *Could* it be that he had condemned her to the irksomeness of boarding school life?"

"Perhaps I should substitute slaves," he joked on. "The twins, you know. They always do the lackeying, and to see *you* taking it on made me wonder if they had gone on strike for once.

22

But put that basket down and come and see Tommy a minute. I've just been changing the dressing on his leg. I don't think he'll be crippled by it for long."

Forgotten for a time, in her love for her horse, was the load of trouble which had been weighing on Rita's mind. With her father's comradely hand at her elbow, she eagerly entered the stable, to be greeted by a delighted whinny from her equine friend.

"Dear old Tommy boy," she crooned, patting his glossy neck and then, while the animal affectionately nuzzled her shoulder, an animated debate went on about his wound, Tommy having come to grief a day or two before through his own exuberance. Capering about a field when out to grass, he had caught the back of one of his shoes in the bottom wire of a fence, and ere his frightened whinnies had brought rescuers to release him, he had thrown himself by his own nervous struggles and cut a foreleg rather badly.

"He will need watching for a while, and, of course, he mustn't be ridden for some little time," Mr. Conway said presently, adding in a rather hurried way, as if to get rid of an unpleasant task; "but he'll get the needed rest without putting you out at all. We've decided to send you away to boarding school for a year or two, girlie, and by the end of your first term Tommy will be all ready for you again, as well as ever."

With hateful remembrance surging back, the girl faced her father passionately.

"School! Oh, *no*, Daddy! I want to stay here with Tommy and everybody. I should *hate* school."

Mr. Conway's face changed suddenly from joviality to sternness. He had snatched at this opportunity of getting through the worst of an anticipated tussle with Rita out of her mother's presence, and he was not minded to let the chance escape him. The matter should be thrashed out here and now.

"Don't be foolish, Rita," he adjured rather impatiently. "You have no possible justification for saying that you will hate school; you haven't even tried it yet. I quite understand that you will miss your freedom at first, but fresh interests will make up for that; you'll make friends and

24

have fine times. It will be a new life for you."

Petulance was in Rita's tone and expression as she retorted:

"But I don't *want* a new life, Daddy. The farm one is good enough for me. I love it."

"Well, you can come back to it when you've finished with school. Meantime, there will be the holidays," was the unyielding reply that greeted her remonstrance.

"Tommy will miss me, horribly," came another argument, half stifled by the girl's rising passion.

"No doubt. But he shall be well exercised and looked after, I promise you. He and Rex shall be my special care."

"Rex!" Rita echoed, adding swiftly: "Then is Jimmy being bundled off to school, too?"

Wisely ignoring the aggressive way in which the query was couched, Mr. Conway nodded. "Yes! Miss Howard knows of a good one; her brother used to be there."

"She *would!* the interfering thing!" Rita's fierce mumble was not sufficiently low to escape her father's sharp hearing. Quick-tempered

25

himself, his colour deepened in the effort he made to get swift command of himself.

"See here, Rita," he said, very firmly, after a momentary pause. "This idea of school for you is by no means a new one. Your mother and I have talked it over several times, in view of the trouble you have constantly stirred up with the different governesses. I suppose if we had lived more in proximity with other people, sheer shame at the frequency with which they have come and gone, would have forced us sooner to drastic action. To your mother and me, Miss Howard has come as a positive godsend; naturally, on learning her profession, we have talked about educational difficulties here; and now we have taken the course she has advised; as there is luckily a vacancy at her school, you are to start next term and, I'm bound to say it, even though it may sound harsh to your ears, in my opinion, Miss Howard's advice didn't come a day too soon. You're kicking over the traces, Rita, and you know it. Now, my dear," here his voice softened considerably, "let's pull together over the matter. You've lots of horse sense when you choose to use it, and you'll realize that upsets won't alter things, but will only cause a lot of unhappiness."

Unhappiness! It was a word quite foreign to the young people of Priory Farm, and it acted like a red rag to a bull on Rita's wrath. If unhappiness was in store, it would be all through that meddlesome Miss Howard. Up to the present, there had been none. Rita exempted even the governesses in that respect. She was quite sure in her own mind that they derived actual satisfaction from the meting out of punishments. And corrective measures had always been regarded by the young Conways as part of the day's work, an aggravation to be borne, but certainly nothing to cause unhappiness.

But this interference of Miss Howard's was different. It was rendering Rita definitely unhappy, so the only thing to do was to make other people the same; in spite of what her father had just said, she still held the hope that if she stirred up enough opposition, the decision would be altered. So, with furious eyes, she faced her father.

"You don't seem to care a bit, Daddy," she

fumed, "how miserable I am going to be, sent away from all the jolliness here. I'd never have believed that you would listen to one of those wretched women who never like girls to enjoy themselves, but are only content when they are marching out all dressed up, in 'crocodiles.'"

Had the situation been less serious, Mr. Conway would have been tempted to laughter over the last scornfully spoken sentence of Rita's tirade; as it was, it only had the effect of showing him what he was up against, in girlish arrogance and self-will. He could tell that his wife's patience and his own self-control were going to be tried to the uttermost if he did not put his foot down here and now.

Chillingly he said: "You are doing no good by this exhibition of rebellion, Rita. Let me tell you this. Upon your behaviour rests the question of Tommy continuing to belong to you. If——"

He was fiercely interrupted. "Nobody can take Tommy away from me, whatever I do. He was Grandpa's present to me and——"

"True," she was interrupted in her turn,

"and I should be very sorry to have to request his recall. But don't forget the message that came with him, Rita. Your grandfather said he expected of you what he would expect of Tommy, that you would 'run straight and take your fences well.' You're not doing it, my girl; you're showing a nasty temper and jibbing outrageously, and I'll not allow a good horse to remain in the ownership of anyone with those vices if I can prevent it."

"But you can't!" flashed Rita. "I'm not nasty tempered with Tommy, ever. He loves me and Grandpa wouldn't take him away from me, I'm sure."

Mr. Conway made no verbal reply to that defiance. He had shot the one bolt that might be expected to take effect upon Rita's wayward-ness, and he closed the argument on his side with a shrug and an abrupt turning away from her, so that she could think over his threat. But before he had reached the stable door, she was past him.

"I shall write to Grandpa myself and tell him everything," was the challenge she flung over her shoulder at her father, and without stopping to retrieve the tea basket, she sped away on winged feet.

Mr. Conway let out a sigh as he watched her flying figure. His hopes of saving his wife some of the expected rumpus had been quickly dashed. Had he taken the wrong line with his headstrong daughter? But that lurking doubt was thrust out a moment later by the fairly certain conviction that no other course would have met with any better success. Not a governess but had tried cajolery before attempting coercion; not one but had had to confess to failure, sooner or later, with the fiery Rita. Mr. Conway decided, therefore, that his attitude towards her had been forced upon him. Her waywardness must be checked now for her own good and for the future peace of her home. However, best let her present temper fizzle out a bit, he thought, before saying any more. So he made no move to follow her, endeavouring instead to let his own vexation simmer down, ere he should again come into contact with her. With that end in view, he gave a pat of extra warmth to the so suddenly deserted Tommy, and set off for a ride round the farm.

Too furious even to think clearly, Rita's first dash took her almost automatically in the direction of her juniors again, though she did not actually approach them at once. A kind of blind rage possessed her, urging her to action, yet preventing her from being conscious of her surroundings or of what she was doing.

Jimmy and the twins, left without their chieftainess, had lazed for a while in the barn after her departure, speculating on the threatening upheaval and her chances of averting it. But at length their minds turned to the games which had been planned.

"We'd better hop along and see which way the wind is blowing," Jimmy decreed, lunging out of his straw nest. "Come along, kids! Let's hope Rita has been able to wangle things."

But, reaching the doorway, he pulled up short in it, staring outwards.

"Whew! she's gone batty. Going round in circles, absolutely," he pronounced.

The twins were beside him in an instant, gazing as wide-eyed as he at the galloping Rita, surging round a duck pond a little distance away.

"Perhaps she's made things all right; perhaps

it's just a sort of Hallelujah caper," ventured Poppy hopefully.

"Whoo! look at her face! There's no Hallelujah on that; it's positively berserk," Jimmy cried, as the said face came more into view; then he gave a cautionary bellow: "Hi! looney! stop it or you'll drop in your tracks!"

Three hearts sank as she veered from her mad plunge round the soft bank of the pond and made for the barn. Never in all their experience had Jimmy and the twins seen such concentrated fury in their sister, accustomed though they were to her stormy nature. So the upheaval was surely coming! It was quite plain that Rita had been assured of that by somebody.

"I say! calm down a bit, old girl," Jimmy exhorted, with real concern, adding as she pulled up before them, panting hard: "Whom did you see? Mummy?"

Her gaze, tormented looking, flicked from one to another in the sympathetic trio; she shook her head.

"No! Daddy!" she jerked out, going on venomously as she got breath enough: "Oh-h-h! I could have *hit* him!"

32

Shocked silence held the others in thrall. Shock, not at the sentiment expressed, but that something should have happened to provoke it. For Mr. Conway was always regarded by his children as such a "chum"; they thought the world of him; never until now, had anything occurred to rouse anger or defiance in either one of them against him; it seemed fantastic, somehow. The twins felt awed, as if the world might be coming to an end.

But Jimmy, boy-like, came to defence of his father after a moment or so.

"No good blaming Dad too much, Rita," he said sturdily. "He's been jockeyed into this business; you know how women can talk and talk, getting round a chap in no time. It's that Howard creature's doing; and with mother agreeing, of course Dad's helpless."

"Then he oughtn't to be," flashed Rita heatedly. "He should have a mind of his own; he should understand better than anybody what the farm life means to us; he loves it and he knows how we love it. To drive any of us away is a—a crime! He says you are to go, too, Jimmy."

c   33

The twins groaned in unison, but the boy only shrugged his shoulders. The news, though unwelcome enough, was half expected. Still, it was of no use fanning Rita's wrath by losing his own temper over matters.

"Oh, well! I suppose if you're going, I might as well go, too," he told Rita, with what she considered maddening placidity.

"Do you mean to say you intend to take it in *that* tame fashion? Aren't you going to fight for your freedom?"

He shrugged again. "What's the use?" he returned doggedly. "If Dad has come to a decision, it's all U.P. I don't mind putting up a fight when there's a sporting chance of winning it, but I don't see much sense in it when I *know* I'll be bested."

Rita's goldy eyes were full of scorn. Allied with anger against her parents, there was now disgust with her brother, and dismay that he would not join her in open revolt.

"So you're going to give in as easily as all that?" Her tone was biting and the boy winced at it. "It's just laziness on your part, Jimmy, sheer laziness. You don't really want the bother

34

of kicking up a row. But you always have been too easy-going."

Jimmy looked stubborn. "Can't help it," he retorted. "Perhaps it's as well that we aren't all such firebrands as you are. As I said just now, I object to fighting when I *know* I'll have to give in. I hate to look a fool."

Rita surveyed him in a grim silence for quite half a minute. She looked as though she would like to shake him. However, she kept her twitching fingers under control, just sneering bitterly at last:

"You'd sooner look a coward! Pah!" Then she flung on her heel and careered off again, leaving a ruffled Jimmy and the twins wailing lamentations over upset fun.

CHAPTER II

FRICTION AND FAILURE

IT was with no very clear idea of what she really intended to do, that Rita pounded along to the house. Seething rage at what she considered a quite unnecessary curtailment of her liberty, kept her brain in a whirl. Certainly she did not feel in a state for letter-writing, in spite of her boast, and even if she had done so, doubts came assailing her now as to which side her grandfather would take. Even though, as his first grandchild, she had always ranked high in his favour, that was no criterion of his backing in this instance. She knew that he had more partiality for young people who excelled in outdoor pursuits, than for those of bookish inclinations, but even so, perhaps he would share her parents' view that school was the thing for a year or two. If he did, his idea of her "running straight and taking her fences well" would take the form of a cheery

36

accordance with their wishes and a passable school record.

"But *that* would never happen," ran her scathing thought on the latter point. "I should be kicking over the traces all the time; I simply couldn't help it." In that frame of mind she shot over the threshold of the home she was so loth to leave, intent on reaching her own room and in one of its thatched gables, to think out in solitude, arguments with which to strengthen her case against school.

That desire was side-tracked, however, by the sight of her mother pausing to look back from a doorway at the back of the spacious tiled hall.

"Mummy! wait a minute!"

Solitude was forgotten in the desire to try for an ally in her father's absence; Rita crossed the hall with swift strides and one look at the girl's fiery expression convinced Mrs. Conway that the school project was already known to her.

"I've just seen Daddy. He says I'm to go to school. To that hateful Miss Howard's school, too, of all places. I loathe the very idea of it, and her, the interfering wretch!"

"Rita! Rita!" But Mrs. Conway's tone of remonstrance put no more than a momentary stopper upon the flood of passionate words. Rita raged on:

"I can't help it, Mummy. It's true. You know it's true, and you ought to be *glad* that I love home too much to want to leave it. You'd have reason to complain if I were aching to get away from it, and you. Instead, I'm aching to stay. Oh, Mummy! *do* persuade Daddy to let me. I'll help in the house, do *anything*, rather than go to school."

Mrs. Conway had been on her way to the dairy, to attend to matters which had already been held up by Miss Howard's visit. But she realized at once that her work would still have to wait awhile. So she closed the door leading into the long passage that ran the whole length of the back of the house, and drew her daughter along with her into the beautiful old, oak-beamed sitting-room, through whose diamond-paned windows floated the sounds which are music in the ears of the country lover, the plaintive baa-ing of lambs and the gentle lowing of cattle.

"Let's talk the matter over quietly here, Rita," Mrs. Conway said. "You know, dear, your own words convince me of the wisdom of our decision regarding school. You would do anything rather than go, you say. Yes! anything to get your own way. That's what it amounts to, put quite plainly. But, dearie, you *must* see reason. None of us can go through the world just taking our own course always. We all have to do things we don't like sometimes. And you only *imagine* that you're going to dislike school. I'm perfectly certain that you will come home after the first term quite keen to go back, even though you've enjoyed a holiday tremendously. There's a heap of fun to be had; there are jolly girls to meet. *I* found it so, and I'm sure you will, too. Some of the girls you will probably make fast friends of, as I did. So be sensible about it, dearie. Daddy and I only want to do our best for you."

Rita's face set in sullen lines. " But school *wouldn't* be the best for me," she argued stubbornly. "I should feel awful and *be* awful, cooped up in one."

Mrs. Conway's heart sank. She had hoped

that Rita would be sufficiently excited by the novelty of complete change to sample it willingly, and so avoid friction. But no! things were going to be difficult, she could see; her own patience and that of her husband promised to be sorely tried before the day of Rita's departure came.

For the first time, the farmer's wife deplored her exacting life, its multitudinous duties always having hindered her from exercising as much personal control over her children's behaviour as she would have liked. However, regrets could not alter matters, she told herself, and as Rita had been headstrong and wilful even as a child, a battle of wills would probably have been inevitable sooner or later, in any case.

Well, now that it *had* come, the battle must be as strategic as she could make it. Thinking thus, she smothered her dismay and remarked quietly but firmly: "You are wanted to help me here later on, Rita. To do that, you must learn all you can, make yourself interesting, so that you can converse well, entertain people and so on. If you are going to grow up a

positive country bumpkin, you won't be capable
of doing any of it. You will be nothing but
a bore, to yourself as well as to others. You
must have something in your head besides a
knowledge of dogs and horses and farming
matters. The more your intellect is developed,
the more you'll appreciate the country life you
love; you will realize all the better how tremendously worth while it is. Whereas, if
Daddy and I were to let you vegetate here
through all your growing up, you would be
dull and discontented presently, and *we* should
be to blame. Try to see our point of view,
dear. We don't *want* to send you away; we
love to have all our children around; but change
and excellent teaching are necessary for your
own good."

She paused to study the effect of her little
homily, having carefully refrained from men-
tioning that which her listener was most in
need of, discipline. But her tact did not win
the reward it merited. Rita scowled, and her
response came rebelliously as ever.

"It all comes to this, Mummy. The Howard
creature is out to boost her school and get

41

pupils for it wherever she can, and she has just talked you and Daddy into the idea of packing me off there. Her holidays are prowling stunts; she just wormed her way in here and was as nice as anything to you and Daddy on purpose to get fees out of you for her old school. No wonder she has seemed to have an eye on me especially whenever she has come. I was to be grist to her mill. Ugh!"

Mrs. Conway had difficulty in resisting a smile.

"You are being absolutely ridiculous, Rita," she said. "Camberside is *not* Miss Howard's school; she is simply the English mistress there, and it is no part of her job to tout for pupils, even if she wished to do such a thing, which is quite unthinkable. As a matter of fact, she is probably only too glad to forget all about troublesome girls when on holiday. That she noticed you were in need of more control than you have had hitherto, I am not surprised, and it was perfectly natural that she should suggest school when I mentioned the difficulty we were having about governesses."

"Because of *me*, I suppose you told her?" was Rita's ruthless interruption.

"I certainly had to admit the truth, ashamed though I was of it," her mother replied with more sharpness than she had yet used. "But I was forced to explain *why* Daddy and I could not get a governess to stay for any length of time. It was no use beating about the bush when we were trying to enlist her help. She has been able to recommend us another governess for the twins, but Daddy and I both feel that this new one must be given a fair chance with them, so you and Jimmy are to go to school."

Rita snatched at an argument here; Priory Farm, although prosperous, required unremitting hard work to make it so.

"It will be frightfully expensive, paying two lots of school-fees and a governess as well," was her tartly spoken reminder.

"I expect we shall survive the expense," Mrs. Conway countered; "and Rita," here she put her hands on the girl's shoulders and spoke with feeling, "no amount of money would compensate Daddy and me for wild and intractable children; remember that."

But Rita backed away from the caressing mother touch.

43

"What I shall remember is that even *you* want to get rid of me, Mummy," she cried tempestuously, and then, before Mrs. Conway could even begin a remonstrance, she whisked out of the room, dashed through the hall door-way again and fled away towards the home meadows.

A little while later she crouched among the bushy growth of a little spinney, hurriedly dabbing rather red-rimmed eyes with the soothing water of the brook that ran through it.

"There! a little walk in the wind will do the rest," the girl muttered to herself after the refreshing treatment had eased the smarting lids. "By the time we meet I shall be looking quite jaunty."

With that she emerged into the open, to walk in the direction of the woman whose sauntering by the waterside she had been watching.

"Lucky I saw her coming," was her self-congratulatory thought. "Now for battle three!" and with the assurance afforded by her certainty that no argus eyes would detect signs of her

44

recent tears, she advanced upon the approaching Miss Howard.

That lady, all unaware of the cyclonic state of the girl, only saw in this lone encounter a rare opportunity for a disarming tête-à-tête. Hitherto, she had talked with the Conway junior element only *en masse*, when the twins had had the most to say, Jimmy and his elder sister having been what could best be described as "stand-offish." Indeed, the younger pair had been mildly indignant at having been obliged to keep up appearances by a more or less continuous babble, to camouflage what was to them a rather embarrassing taciturnity on the part of the other two. Not that they wanted to be affable to Miss Howard; they were in perfect agreement with Rita that teachers were "all of a kidney" and therefore to be treated as scurvily as one dared, but they had not reached the age when lofty scorn sat easily, as it did upon the elder girl. Besides, if Miss Howard had been anybody but a member of the obnoxious profession, they would not have wilfully blinded themselves to the fact that she looked and could be, quite charming.

45

In the present circumstances, the smile with which she greeted Rita might well have melted a heart less obdurate. But the girl saw in it only the triumph of a woman who had got her way, and she accordingly resented it all the more bitterly. Therefore eyes as steady as they were hostile, repulsed Miss Howard's attempt at friendliness. Studying the girl in whose path she stood, the woman felt a sudden stab of dismay that anyone so pretty could look so utterly repulsive. Rita's riot of short auburn curls made a frame for a positive picture face, that kept its fascinatingly clear red and white through all weathers, the curls falling over the forehead almost to the strongly marked eyebrows.

"Unusually pretty; she'll have quite a vogue at school if she doesn't upset everybody by ill temper," was Miss Howard's unspoken comment as she gazed at the pupil-to-be and made another attempt to win her confidence.

"Isn't it lovely in these meadows? How I shall miss them when I have to go back into a town. You are lucky, Rita, to have a home in such peaceful and healthy surroundings."

46

The words were meant to placate; they had the directly opposite effect, giving Rita a lead for her truculence.

"If you think that, Miss Howard," she retorted witheringly, "why couldn't you have left me to enjoy it? Why did you come here urging Mummy and Daddy to send me away from it?"

Miss Howard's eyebrows went up in genuine astonishment at this attack. "But, my *dear!* I didn't urge anything. I merely offered advice when it was asked for. And after all, Rita, school is only a matter of a few weeks at a time. You'll have all the holidays at home."

The girl's goldy eyes had a tigerish gleam in them.

"Holidays!" Indignation choked her on the word, but after a quick swallow she went on: "School means three quarters of the year away. And there's something here for every hour of every day of every week."

"Well!" Miss Howard was stung into sharp rejoinder by the girl's tone and expression. "So there will be at school."

"Not the things *I* care for—horses, dogs,

47

animals and jobs of *all* kinds, riding to hounds, things like that, that count. And— freedom!"

The clipped, passionate utterances held a fierce challenge, and they were followed by a tense silence, during which Miss Howard stared a trifle dazedly at the young spitfire. Difficult and temperamental girls she had encountered in plenty during her three years' experience, but never one of Rita's blatant ferocity, and she had to admit herself definitely worried.

But it would never do to let Rita suspect her of dismay, flashed the swift thought that made her pull herself together and answer quietly:

"Of course, Rita, there will be none of your pet distractions in school life. You will *have* to part with them for a while, as well as, yes! your freedom too. Still, there will be compensa- tions——"

"Lessons, games, lessons, bed; day in and day out. Oh, yes, great compensations; most *thrilling* compensations," came the sarcastic interruption.

The very truth it contained made answer

difficult, but Miss Howard gamely took up the challenge.

"There *is* a certain amount of monotony, Rita, I admit," she said; "routine is apt to make us chafe at times, but it is very necessary in our lives, all the same. My dear, I'm sure you will enjoy school if you make up your mind to do so. After all, I speak from experience. I *loved* my time at boarding school."

"Did you leave a place like this for it?"

"Well, no! I can't say *that*," Miss Howard answered the quick question rather regretfully. "You see, although I am living in a rather nicer place now on account of—er—my mother's health, my home has always been in town."

"Then you can't possibly speak from an experience like mine," cut in the girl with finality. "I shall detest your school and everybody in it if I'm made to go to it. But I won't let that happen without a big fight."

Miss Howard's usually pleasant face hardened. Rita had managed what she had deliberately set out to accomplish, a weakening of the other's self-control. In ironical triumph she saw Miss Howard's colour rise angrily and her blue eyes flash, flinging away from her then with a shrug and a malicious grin.

"You are a most disagreeable girl, Rita," Miss Howard called sharply after her, "and if you are going through the world in this fashion, you will find it a very hard place."

But Rita merely shrugged her shoulders disdainfully again as she marched off. Miss Howard had been shown what she was letting herself in for by touting for pupils, and that was *that*! She was welcome to the last word, the girl cynically decided. Rita had no more time to spare for baiting her at present, having suddenly come to a decision that sent her hastening back to the farmhouse.

She emerged from it soon with the same stealth with which she had entered; but her appearance was changed. In place of her short skirt and jumper, she word jodhpurs and riding coat, the boyish apparel suiting her lithe, slim figure to perfection.

It was such a "second nature" garb to Rita, however, that she did not even think of her appearance, her mind being centred upon getting away upon an errand of her own without being questioned and stopped.

Regretful thoughts of her own much-prized mount were quickly soothed by her success in borrowing Rex, Jimmy's pony, without being seen, and very soon, she was giving him rein for a smart gallop over the heath on a ten mile ride.

"I'll get first innings with Grandpa, any-how," she told herself resolutely. "Pity I didn't think of this before, instead of wasting time blubbing. But I can say all I want and be back again before dark, if I'm quick. I should have been heard if I'd tried 'phoning, and a letter would have taken me ages. Much better to *see* Grandpa."

Lurking under that last thought was its *real* meaning, that it was much better for wheedling purposes that Grandpa should see *her*. She knew that he kept the softest spot in his heart for his grand-children, and that she had her special niche. Wheedling had answered many a time before; perhaps it would do so again; and Mummy and Daddy were always a good deal influenced by Grandpa's opinion.

With renewed hope as these facts occurred to her, Rita let the pony work off his first freshness by the gallop, and then settled him down to the steady canter more suited to the safety of wind and limb, pulling up presently at the door of her grandfather's house with the rousing "Tally-ho!" that never failed to attract his attention if he were within.

Rita had been pretty sure of her quarry; her grandfather's evening habits were mostly of the pipe and wireless variety. He had retired from farming after his son's marriage, glad to leave the Priory Farm in the hands of a new master and mistress after the loss of his own wife. In an old-world house in a still old-world village, he made a sanctuary for himself and a widowed niece, getting activity and interest out of his hobby as master of fox-hounds, and endless diversion from the doings of his grandchildren.

But a rather startled look clouded his usually whimsical expression as he stood framed in his doorway a minute later, eyeing the unexpected caller.

"What's afoot? Anything wrong? Eh?" was his bluff query.

"I just want to talk to you a bit specially, Grandpa. But I mustn't be long; and Rex wants a drink, so shall we chat in the yard?"

Rita's eyes, a-sparkle from her ride, cajoled the old stalwart out to walk at her stirrup till, with the stable yard reached, she dismounted and left Rex in safety to his own devices, while she broached her errand.

"Grandpa! you'd hate me to be unhappy, wouldn't you?"

"Desperately," he replied lightly, but with a wary eye upon her.

"Then, Grandpa, will you stop Mummy and Daddy from sending me away to school?"

He puffed out his cheeks dubiously at that, slowly shaking his head at last.

"Beyond my province, my dear, I'm afraid. You belong to them, you know, not to me; and my son isn't a boy now, remember, to have the law laid down for him by his father."

"But he'd listen to advice from you, Grandpa; he always does; you could persuade him."

Another shake of the old man's head. "Not

53

against what he considered his better judgment, Rita," he demurred. "My son, your father, isn't like that. You know it."

The "devil's tattoo" of the girl's riding crop against her leg grew more impatient.

"But you said you'd hate me to be unhappy," she persisted.

"And I repeat, desperately." There was no mistaking the deep affection in the face he bent to her. "But why should you be unhappy, child? School isn't a prison."

"It will be, to me," she flashed. "Oh, Grandpa! surely you understand. You've never refused me anything I've asked before. Grandpa !"

She knew she had shaken him by that last wistful appeal; that he found the pleading in the face and voice of his favourite all but irresistible. But sneaking hope was killed an instant later.

"No! I don't believe I have, Rita, but I expect I ought to have done, sometimes. Perhaps if I had, it wouldn't be so hard for us both now, for me to refuse and for you to be refused. The time comes, you know, my dear," here he gave her his whimsical smile, "when we've all got to be broken in to the collar, but it's a nicer and an easier job for the human colts of these days than it was for those of *my* youth. You'll be settling down and thoroughly enjoying school in a brace of shakes."

If he had looked for a softening of the flinty young face under his kindly tone, he was disappointed. As though she had not heard him, she said hardly:

"Daddy threatened that you would take Tommy back again if I jibbed. *Would* you?"

The old man wagged a protesting head at her. "You're putting me between the devil and the deep sea with that question, Rita," was the evasion which he trusted would dissuade her from pushing the inquiry farther.

She would have none of that, however.

"*Would* you, Grandpa?" she reiterated stubbornly, and he saw that he would have to seem cruel to be kind.

"D'you remember the condition Tommy carried with him, Rita? Well," as she gave a reluctant nod, "*that's* my answer; but, Rita, to see Tommy back in my stables would be one of the saddest sights of my life." He paused a moment, then added very quietly: "You aren't going to let that happen, my girl, are you?"

Dumbly she searched his face for a sign of relenting, then a headshake gave the answer he wanted, the answer that she could not trust herself to put into words. Grandpa had been her last hope and he had failed her. She had lost her fight for her own way.

CHAPTER III

MISSING

ALL unwittingly, however, old Mr. Conway put into Rita's hand before she left, something that again fostered within her the hope of resistance.

"You must come along inside a minute and say how-do to your aunt," he said after a moment or so, anxious to break up a painful and hitherto unheard-of constraint between them. "I should never hear the last of it if you went off without the usual lemonade and biscuits. Rex is enjoying his light refreshment; thinks he has earned it, no doubt."

Only consideration for the pony weighed with Rita; she was feeling too sore and thwarted to want to exchange chit-chat, even with her kindly aunt.

"But I can't take it out of Rex just because I'm wretched myself," was her private thought, so she left him contentedly champing some hay

57

he had nosed out, while she paid the brief duty call.

Her grandfather had had something beside refreshment in mind, however, when proposing the adjournment to the house. A visit to his own room and the rattle of a cashbox lid, resulted in something crackly being squeezed into one of Rita's palms after she had mounted Rex once more.

"A five pound note, my dear, to stow safely into a pocket," her grandfather said, smiling encouragingly up at her. "You'll probably need a new tennis racquet and so on for school. Anyhow, use the money for a new games outfit or anything else you're specially wanting. It can be a bit on account of what I've planned to give you when you come of age."

A sop to his conscience, that last sentence! Rita knew as well as he did himself, that the money was intended to ease the situation. Gilding the school pill, came the girl's swift thought; which was none the less bitter, for it was the one that instantly followed. Still, Grandpa meant to be kind; she loved him for that even though she wanted to thrust the money back. But looking down at him, she hadn't the heart to do it straight away. She would keep it a day or two and then *send* it back, telling him that she wouldn't need a new racquet or anything, because she wouldn't feel like playing games at a school; she wouldn't be happy enough for that if she had to go.

If she had to go! That mental reservation kept reiterating in her brain for long after she had soberly thanked her grandfather and left him feeling rather downcast. Never before in all her young life had he seen his favourite look as she did now, and when she was out of sight he wended his way indoors with the somewhat sad reflection that Priory Farm would seem a dull place while she was away from it. School! he shook his head, more than a little doubt in his mind as to her success in one. Who could wonder that such a wild, free thing as she was should look upon school life as a cribbed, cabined and confined existence? Well! well! it had to be and he hoped she would make the best of it.

The object of his thoughts was setting Rex a very different pace from the eager one of a short time before. She rode slowly, pondering, with one hand thrust into the pocket in which the bank note reposed. It was now opening up in Rita's mind the possibility of further rebellion against the school mandate.

"Anything I'm specially wanting, Grandpa said," she muttered as she fingered the bank note. "Well, I'm specially wanting to keep my freedom, and if his money will help to scare Mummy and Daddy into letting me, he won't blame me for using it that way; in the bottom of his heart he won't, anyway, whatever he might feel obliged to pretend. And he wouldn't take Tommy back for good; I'm sure he wouldn't. Five pounds! I can give Mummy and Daddy the biggest scare of their lives with it; they'll see how desperate I am. I'll do it! Yes, I'll do it!"

As if to keep pace with her hurrying thoughts, she urged Rex into a canter after that, restraining him only when nearing the farm. Then, having set him free again in the paddock, she made the most of the growing dusk to collect certain things she wanted from the house. Ten minutes or so later, she dropped a tightly packed knapsack from her bedroom window, following

it from the low sill into the seclusion of the
fruit garden by way of a massive old fig tree
that grew against that side of the house. Then,
under cover of gooseberry and currant bushes,
she gained the orchard, where she changed her
riding coat for a farm smock, emerging soon
from the orchard to go padding along a wide
cart track across the fields.

"The village is out of the question," she
said to herself, "but in the bus and at the
junction station, I shall pass muster all right
in this light, I think. Anyhow, if I can catch
the express, I shall make a good get-away before
the hue and cry begins."

Luck certainly favoured the truant and her
crazy scheme. Seated presently in the dining
car of a thundering express train, she ate her
dinner with the greatest gusto, studying meanwhile an advertisement which was part of her
runaway equipment and which, in fact, had
made the idea of flight a possible one. The
advertisement, which had happened to catch
her eye in one of the farm journals that very
morning, was for several young assistants on
a goat farm near a town some fifty miles away.

"These Lornes are pretty sure to be sporting sort of women if they like animals," Rita mused comfortably apropos the advertisers, "and as it isn't *every* farm girl who is fond of pernickety goats, I think I'm safe for a job. Then I shall write to Mummy and Daddy and say I'd sooner be an exile from home earning my living, than at a school. *That* ought to bring everybody to heel. If it doesn't, well! I shall stick my toes in and stay on with the goats. No prodigal son business for me!"

It was her profound confidence in herself that carried the day. When panic was reigning at Priory Farm a little later that evening, she was calmly interviewing the rather puzzled but definitely attracted goat farmers. They were a middle-aged woman and her mother, who were divided between concern at such a late arrival of a youthful applicant and amusement at her absolute assurance.

"I love goats and I can manage them," she said; "we've always kept them at home, so when I saw your advertisement to-day, I decided to come to you for work, as I'm needing a job badly."

The goat-ladies had been studying intently this visitor who had descended upon them from the last bus of the day to their quiet neighbourhood. Here was the kind of girl they wanted on their farm, robust-looking, well-spoken; the kind whom it would be a pleasure to have about them. She was young, having owned to only fourteen years, but she looked capable and workmanlike in her breeches and smock. The Lornes wanted several of their helpers to live at the farm, and this applicant had already expressed her wish to do so. She looked frank-faced, honest; they liked her appearance immensely. Still, there *were* the necessary formalities attaching to employment to be observed; the matter of a reference, for one thing.

Tactfully the younger woman began more intimate questioning.

"You still *have* your home, I suppose?"

"Oh, yes!" was the girl's ready answer. "But it's quite a way from here; between forty and fifty miles, I believe."

The questioner was evidently startled, but she nodded gravely and resumed consideringly:

"I see! that accounts for your lateness in coming here, perhaps? You didn't see the advertisement in time to apply earlier?"

The girl's eyes were quite unwavering as she replied:

"Oh, yes, I saw it this morning, though I didn't decide to come until this evening."

"But what arrangements did you make with your people? You see, my mother and I feel a certain responsibility. You must stay here to-night, of course, but that cannot be taken as a guarantee that we shall employ you. I quite *think* you will prove suitable, but we shall have to make a few inquiries, naturally. You have parents alive, I hope?"

Rita saw that all her resource would be called into play at this juncture. Truthfulness was necessary in order to carry conviction, but it must be cloaked to a certain extent or her scheme might be upset too soon for it to have any effect upon the school plan. So, carefully, she felt her way.

"Oh yes, I have parents," she admitted, adding with a disarming little smile: "but they are not very pleased with me at the moment,

64

though that's not really my fault. I'd better be quite straight with you about it, then perhaps you'll help me. You see, I'm crazy to do farming and—er—all that, and they want me to do quite different kind of work that I hate, so I thought I would just get a job first, of the kind I wanted, and when they see I'm really settling down to it, they'll agree all right that it's the best thing for me. If you'll just keep me here on trial for two or three days, and you find I'll suit, I shall be able to write and tell them at home how happy I am."

"But, in the meantime, your parents will be anxious about you, surely?"

Rita shrugged. "A bit, of course, but it won't be for long. They'll soon hear from me."

"What life is it that they wish you to lead?" the look accompanying that question was very searching, but the girl did not flinch.

"A stuffy indoor one, mostly, and it would kill me!" she replied with sudden heat.

Mother and daughter exchanged glances. The situation was distinctly disturbing yet, lovers of outdoor pursuits themselves, they had every sympathy with the girl whose craving for them was apparently being thwarted. There were parents who tried to impose unsuitable careers upon their children. Probably those in this case wished their daughter to go in for office work or something of the kind. Foolish, of course, when anyone could see that the girl was a typically outdoor specimen.

"Let me see! What did you say your name is?" the younger woman inquired suddenly.

But Rita was not to be caught napping. She had given her two middle names upon arrival and was not trapped by the abrupt demand into confessing to anything different.

"Joan Wilson!" she repeated with absolute confidence.

"Well, then, Joan, you must stay here to-night, as I said," Miss Lorne continued. "I manage the actual business and my mother the household part of the farm, but she and I must talk over you before deciding anything. You're a bit of a problem, you know. However, you're probably tired now, so we won't rub that in too much to-night. Trot along with my mother and she'll see you comfortably bedded."

66

Neither strangeness, excitement over her escapade, nor the uncertainty of the morrow, had much effect on the sleeping powers of the health-abounding Rita. She slept soundly, awoke in the morning with the lark and was out helping with the early milking of the goats, looking as fresh as the dew and the opening daisies.

The goat farmers beamed appreciatively at her over the early breakfast. Privately wondering to what decision they had arrived concerning herself, she kept up a lively conversation with them and another assistant they had already taken on, airing her knowledge of goats and their little ways with an easy simplicity that showed her completely *au fait* on the subject of their management and welfare.

And as if everything were conspiring to aid and abet the runaway, just as the meal had finished an urgent telephone message from the county hospital for a supply of milk sent Miss Lorne racing off in her car at a moment's notice, and Rita, aware that her fate had been forgotten in the sudden bustle, slipped from the house with an inward chuckle, following the other farm girl out to further duties with the herd.

67

Occupied with the day's orders and a multitude of other matters, the older woman gave no further thought to Rita until they met at lunch time.

"Good gracious!" she exclaimed then. "I'd completely forgotten about you for the time being. And my daughter won't be home until evening. She has a market to attend and several business calls to make besides. Dear! dear! and we hadn't quite decided what to do about you."

"Oh, well! to-morrow will be soon enough," Rita broke in hastily. "A few hours more won't matter so far as I'm concerned, and they'll give you a little time to see how I'm likely to shape." Then she adroitly switched attention from herself to farm details, making inquiries that successfully directed Mrs. Lorne's thoughts into other channels.

Later that day luck seemed to be favouring Rita again. A telephone message came from Miss Lorne to the effect that the car had broken down, she would be delayed for repairs and could not be home till very late.

So Rita went to bed that second night at the goat farm, with the sublime hope that she had scored all along the line over Miss Howard's machinations.

But her triumph had a sharp uprooting next day.

A paragraph in the morning paper, lying open from a hasty scanning by one of the goat-ladies, caught Rita's eye as she bent to move the newspaper from her chair, and "Oh!" she cried out involuntarily.

The attention of the others drawing up to the breakfast table was immediately focussed upon her, and Miss Lorne suddenly rushed round to the new arrival, exclaiming:

"Whatever is the matter, child? What have you seen?"

Pale and strangely stricken-looking was the face Rita lifted to her.

"I must go home. Grandpa's ill, through me!" she groaned, and pointed to the paragraph which told of Rita Conway's disappearance from Priory Farm and a heart attack brought on by shock and anxiety from which the girl's grandfather was suffering.

"I must go home," she repeated dully, hopelessly. "But may I phone first, *now*?"

69

And a few minutes later Mr. Conway, junior, was listening thankfully to his daughter's voice over the telephone.

"That you, Daddy?" it said, rather shakily, and after explaining the whereabouts of its owner, added: "Tell Grandpa I'm quite safe and well and that I'm coming home at once."

She made a clean breast of the whole affair to the Lornes before she left them.

"You've been very kind to me," she said, "so I feel bound to explain properly," and after doing so and revealing her real identity, she added: "Anyhow, you'll see that I told you the truth after a fashion, so I hope you won't think *too* badly of me."

Kindly smiles assured the girl that she had won a certain amount of sympathy and liking, in spite of her regrettable escapade, and Miss Lorne took the opportunity of offering a word of advice and cheer when she had driven the forlorn, would-be farm girl to the station for her train home.

"You know, my dear," she said, "*I* must confess to having hated the idea of my first boarding school, but, bless you, I was as gay as a lark before I had been in it a week. Girls are mostly adaptable creatures. You just make up your mind to take things as they come; you'll be surprised to find how it helps. And if ever you do want a job in the future, come to me. I'll employ you. But I expect you'll have aspirations far above a goat-girl's duties when your schooldays are done."

Rita hung out of the train, her face rueful.

"Miss Lorne," she cried protestingly, "I'd sooner do the meanest work on your farm, on any farm, than be at school. Good-bye! good-bye! I've made some new friends, anyhow, through running away, and I shall come to see you and your mother and the goats again some day."

The journey back to the junction she had left two days previously, was an uneasy prelude to "facing the music" at Priory Farm, and it was an undeniable relief to Rita to see her father awaiting her arrival at the station.

"One at a time will be easier than having everybody on at me at once," she soliloquised. "They're sure to be frightfully up in arms against me, over the upset to Grandpa."

But one glance at her father's face showed it more grieved than angry.

"I'll take you along to Grandpa before we go home," he said quite quietly to the culprit. "You see, he blamed *himself* for this disgraceful outbreak of yours. If he hadn't given you money, you couldn't have been tempted to such a thing, he said. So we'll get along to him quickly."

Rita nodded, dumb for once in her life, and only once did she break the oppressive silence of the car drive to her grandfather's house.

"Is he better?" she asked huskily.

"Yes, much, since you phoned this morning," was the brief reply she received, and then no other word passed her lips until she stood shamefacedly beside her grandfather.

"I'm sorry, Grandpa, sorry to have upset you so," she said in a low voice, her eyes searching anxiously his slightly pinched features. "But you'll soon be all right again, won't you?"

"Oh yes, I shall now," he assured her. "Just a sudden flop, must take it quietly for a few days, that's all."

She laid a little pile of money on the bed.

"That's the change, Grandpa. From the five pounds, you know. I didn't spend a great lot, and I'll make it up out of my pocket money if you don't mind waiting a bit for it."

Her grandfather gathered the money up and put it on a table by his side.

"Never mind about the balance, Rita. We'll charge that up to experience," he replied. "But I'll take the other back, because you and I both know, don't we, girlie, that it was a sort of bribe really and truly, and bribes aren't good things with which to meddle, are they?"

"No!" agreed Rita tonelessly.

But there was no regret in the girl's mind at having to return the money. After all, she had decided in the first place that she would not keep it, so no feeling of loss attached to it. What did exercise her was the thought of Tommy. What would her grandfather do about the pony in face of an escapade that had made *him* ill, created a furore in the neighbourhood, and even dragged in the police and the newspaper people? Eyeing him narrowly, she swallowed nervously once or twice, then had to moisten lips suddenly dry from fright before she could say, a trifle unsteadily:

"Grandpa! Tommy! Is it all right about him?"

"Tommy?" The old man frowned consideringly as he echoed the name. His mind was still centred in a troubled way upon his error of judgment in having tried to buy Rita into behaving tractably.

But Rita took the frown to mean the worst, and trembled for her most valued possession.

"Oh, Grandpa, not Tommy, too! You won't take him back, too!" she pleaded huskily.

He caught at her meaning then, a flash of recollection reminding him of the bargain struck between them; she feared that this fresh outbreak had cancelled that.

Hastily he murmured: "It's all right, child. I'm not even considering such a thing. We compromised over Tommy, didn't we? Well, I'm not letting this little to-do alter that, because I blame myself for making it possible. No! no! Tommy is yours all right, my dear. So now you pop off home to him and set all our minds at rest by being reasonable."

74

"Thank you, Grandpa!" and "I'll try!" were her subdued responses, and gratitude for his clemency put a fervour into her kiss and a softness into her eyes that gave him new hope of her.

But, unfortunately, the softening was of so transitory a nature that it did not even last out the rest of that day. The look on her mother's face aroused the old irritation at once, not with her mother, but with the cause of all the upset at the farm. Mrs. Conway received the culprit most tactfully, indulging in no actual recrimination, merely murmuring her thankfulness that Rita was safely back, but she could not keep the little break out of her voice, or hide the tired, saddened face that told of a sleepless night of anxiety.

The twins and Jimmy were not so discreet in their reception of the prodigal. They all wore long faces that had more than a hint of reproach for their sister in them, the stress and hubbub following her disappearance having scared them badly. It seemed one thing to talk of serious revolt, but quite another—an unbearable sort of business, in fact—to carry it into action.

75

The atmosphere of panic had jangled their nerves; having witnessed Rita's passion and heard her ragings, their imaginations had simply run riot upon courses she might have taken to escape the banishment to school.

"Oh, Rita, you needn't have frightened us so," was Poppy's half resentful greeting. "Tess and I couldn't help wondering if you had gone mad and jumped down the well-hole or something. We thought the well might have been on your mind a bit after our talking of letting Miss Howard fall down it; you remember."

"I don't believe any of us had one wink of sleep last night," Tessa followed up swiftly. "Mummy cried dreadfully, and Daddy got doctor here at last to give her a dose of something. We've never seen her ill before, and oh, Rita, it was awful! Don't let's any of us make quite such dreadfulness again."

Rita's brows lowered. "You're forgetting the dreadfulness that has been made for me, aren't you?" she remarked bitterly. "You seem to be thinking more of all the upset to yourselves than of what might have happened to me."

Jimmy burst in impatiently at that. "Don't

talk rot, Rita. You know very well the kids didn't mean that. It has been a perfectly frightful bust up, with police and press johnnies buzzing around looking pop-eyed as if they were all hoping for a murder scoop or something else really scandalizing. You can't wonder at our all getting the wind up. Dash it! we didn't want to think of anything awful having happened to you. Grandpa being taken ill, too, frightened us all to fits. Ah! talking of him reminds me; you don't know when you're well off, old girl."

"What do you mean, Jimmy?" Rita demanded, looking down her nose at him.

The boy soon enlightened her. "My word! I only wish that present of five pounds had been offered to me. I'd have spent it on something better than a useless skidaddle."

No doubt it was the last sentence that carried the sting, although Jimmy meant it harmlessly enough.

Rita's eyes sparkled viciously. "Huh!" she retorted with venom. "It would have been 'A Present for a Good Boy,' wouldn't it? And a new cricket bat and so on would have quite shut you up on the subject of school. Well, I'm different; I didn't want hush-money, so I was going to return it in any case. And I *have* given most of it back, because I only spent a little of it on the 'useless skidaddle,' so there, clever!"

After which outburst she made for her own room, in all the greater fume for having realized that further revolt was useless.

So, three weeks later, outwardly subdued, but inwardly seething, a scapegrace went to school.

CHAPTER IV

SURPRISE FOR CAMBERSIDE

A KNOT of Camberside girls, having finished their unpacking for the new term, were enjoying a breather in the school grounds, sauntering along the grassy track that fringed the long drive, their attention alert for later arrivals.

"About this Conway creature who's descending on us," Coral Brand was saying. "Is she a relative of Miss Howard, does anybody know, that she's being flung into the breach at the last minute, so to speak?"

There was a blank silence; nobody *did* know, so after a few moments Coral resumed:

"Because it's through Miss Howard, and with her, that she's coming, and from some region where the former has been rusticating, I hear. H'm! if the girl *is* related, we shall have some snubbing to do; I expect she's sure to take advantage if she happens to be a pet niece or something. Nuisance the vacancy happens to be in our Form; we were pulling along very comfortably together, but we shall have to be jolly careful if this new girl is pally with Miss Howard."

There was a general murmur of assent from her companions, a stranger in their midst was always a disturbing factor, but the advent of one who might be extra eyes and ears for a mistress was all the more unwelcome.

They need not have worried themselves; that fact was borne upon them very soon and very unmistakably, the enlightenment being so swift and so complete that it almost took their breath away. For as it happened, they were all witnesses of the new girl's arrival with the English mistress. The taxi that brought the pair from the station, drawing up behind several others already unloading near the entrance, disgorged its passengers immediately beneath one of the Fourth Form dormitory windows, out of which Coral and her friends were peering inquisitively.

"Well, here we are, Rita," there floated up to them in Miss Howard's very clear voice.

"Welcome to Camberside. I do hope you are going to be happy here."

Then, faces that were wearing amused smirks over this little speech, changed to liveliest astonishment at the reception it received.

"Thanks, Miss Howard," the listeners heard an equally clear and absolutely icy voice say, "but what *is* the use of your hoping that, when you know very well that I'm *not* going to be happy. I shall have to rub along somehow, of course, and at any rate, I won't be starting here as a humbug."

"Whew-w-w-w!" Coral whistled softly, holding her breath again in time to listen with the rest of the flabbergasted audience to a curtly spoken:

"You seem determined to persist in your rudeness, Rita. I can only trust that the humanizing influence of nice girls will create a change in you before long. Move along to the hall door, please, I will be there in a few moments."

Withdrawing their craning necks a minute later, the girls in the dormitory gazed at each other in really comic amaze, tongues seemingly paralysed till Coral broke the spell with:

F   81

"We doubtless being some of the aforesaid 'nice girls'? What about it? My goodness! To think we've lived to see a savage come to Camberside! Whew-w-w-w! Phew-w-w-w! and all that! Fan me, somebody."

But as everybody else was in the same need of restorative measures, the appeal went unheeded.

"She struck me as being a precious good-looking savage, anyhow, from what could be seen of her face under her hat," averred one, Hilary Betterton, who, with Coral, rather led Fourth Form opinion.

"But, girls, the venom in the tongue! My gracious! She must be a relative of Miss Howard's, surely, to have dared such a poisonous dig at her."

A perfect screech of laughter went up, followed by some satirical remarks at Hilary's expense.

"Well, you know what I mean," was her counter-thrust. "Everybody comes out with home truths to relations occasionally. One isn't always one's politest to them, whereas——"

"'Nough said, Hil, you're only exposing

skeletons in your cupboard," interrupted Coral
amid renewed laughter. "Evidently only we
here are privileged to witness your good manners.
Seriously though, you're probably right about
the pretty savage. Has anybody *ever* heard
anybody talk to a real *anybody* as she did?"

Spoken negatives and portentous headshakes
disclaimed any such thing.

"Brazen, absolutely," somebody added.

"Miss Howard's quite a decent sort too,"
was another girl's testimony.

"H'm, yes! It looks quite as though we
shall have to take the savage in hand and teach
her how to behave," Coral said. "None of us
are angels, but she really did sound the limit.
I wonder *why* she's so certain of not liking
Camberside? Well, we shall soon know more
about her. She'll be brought up here before
we've time for much more puzzling."

However, conjecture was not destined to
cease immediately upon the stranger's appearance in the dormitory, where she was presently
heralded by a senior girl.

"Rita Conway, girls! Show her the ropes!"
was all the introduction or help given to either

side, and for a full minute silence reigned while
Rita's wonderful goldy eyes studied the faces
of her schoolmates-to-be with a cool deliberation
that staggered them.

They, in their turn, stood staring at her like
so many startled sheep.

On her way to the dormitory she had pulled
off her hat; Rita hated hats, seldom wore them
and regarded the one she now clutched
ruthlessly, with frightful menace to its brim,
as one of the numerous plagues of school
life.

So Coral and her coterie had an unhampered
view of the auburn mass that so enhanced Rita's
facial prettiness, and frankly admitted to themselves that there wasn't another girl in the
school to touch her. They were prey to such
utter absorption that her voice at last made
most of them jump.

"Heavens! *How* you all stare! Anyone
would think I was a freak," she said, with a
most patent lack of cordiality in her tones.

It nettled Coral. "Well! *You're* staring at
us. Perhaps you think *us* freaks!" she retorted.

"Oh, I've seen worse collections in my time.

84

Quite a lot turn up at the meets, for instance," was the newcomer's laconic statement.

The sheeplike look of her hearers gave place to more individual expressions, some truculent, others amused. But the stranger refused either to wilt under frowns or respond to smiles, as yet. She just stood her ground, quite evidently taking the measure of the girls amongst whom her lot was cast for a time.

However, as it was against all precedent to allow a new pupil *all* her own way, Coral essayed a snub.

"We understood that you were coming from the wilds of somewhere," she remarked cuttingly; "so I suppose we should hardly be surprised at a positive savage with no manners at all, especially as we heard the appalling way you talked to Miss Howard just now."

Rita's glance left the speaker for the adjacent open window, to which, after an instant's pause, she strolled lazily across.

"Humph!" turning back with an insolent smile as she recognised its position. "So you were all spying and eavesdropping. Fine ones *you* are to judge other people's behaviour. But you don't *look* as smug as you sound, so if you'll stop acting as humbugs, I'd rather like to know your names."

Carol swept her a mocking curtsey.

"The desire shall be granted, O monarch from the nether regions," was her sarcastic sally. "Girls!" to her friends, "let each line up and say her little piece with fitting humility to the new queen of the dorm."

The gust of laughter stirred by this repartee, successfully cleared the way for introductions, at any rate. Good-naturedly the old stagers clustered round the new one, chattering their various nomenclatures in her ears until she clapped her hands over those shapely orifices and drawled:

"Hoots! You're like a pack of bidders at a sale. One at a time, *please*; I'll have to sort you out at leisure."

There was no lack of comradely aid when, a few minutes later, Rita's luggage was brought up for bestowal in her cubicle. In fact, the little apartment overflowed with helpers, all suffering from an acute attack of curiosity about the new and decidedly fascinating schoolfellow.

86

And the curiosity grew with the minutes, for to every request for guidance as to where this or that unpacked article should be bestowed, she waved an impatient hand and replied in some such words as: "Oh, shove it anywhere! Squash it in one of the drawers; *I* don't care!"

She had such dainty belongings, too. Mrs. Conway had tried her hardest to brighten Rita's departure from home by a generous supply of the pretty things so acceptable as a rule to girls of her age. But the deposed ruler of the roost at the Priory Farm was too bitter about the clipping of her wings of freedom to be placated by new fine feathers. Her lack-lustre eyes had watched their packing, as now complete boredom attended their unpacking. They might have been so many rags for all Rita appeared to care, and her assistants were immensely puzzled. Even though her response to Miss Howard's welcoming words gave them a clue to her line of conduct, it did not explain why she was so disgruntled at the idea of life at Camberside. But opportunity came at length for Coral to set the question ball rolling.

"Well now, Rita," she began, seating herself on the bed with an air of great determination, "I'd better let you know at the outset that this fighting and helping a new girl to unpack isn't our usual procedure here, but to be perfectly frank, we're all dying to know something. Are you related to Miss Howard?"

"Heaven forbid!" Rita snapped, adding after a moment or so with wide-eyed wonder, "why on earth should you think I might be?"

A relating of the school gossip concerning her soon enlightened Rita on this point, but at the end of the recital she burst out:

"It's certainly true, worse luck, that I travelled from home with Miss Howard; in fact the Meddlesome Matty actually arranged it with the Headmistress here, else she was due back two days ago, to get ready for term time, she said. I could see her game plainly enough; she was afraid that with her out of the way I should be able to get round my people not to send me here after all. So she laid her nice little plan, pretending that it was to save Mummy and Daddy the time and expense of seeing me settled in here, but really it was

88

to make quite sure of me, and to get me under her thumb as quickly as possible, too. Well, she hadn't a chance to enjoy the journey; I saw to *that*. I made myself just as objectionable as I knew how."

"But why in the world?" cut in Hilary abruptly. "What's your particular grudge against her, anyhow, and why all the rumpus about your coming to Camberside? It isn't a lunatic asylum or a leper colony. What's wrong with a mere school?"

The impatiently put question opened a floodgate of Rita's surging wrath.

"*Everything's* wrong!" she fumed, and for the next five minutes nobody else could get a word in edgewise, not that it mattered, the girls might well have comforted themselves, for Rita's rapid tongue gave such a comprehensive summary of her affairs that further questioning was unnecessary; soon the whole brood of listeners were in possession of as much information as was required to give them a thorough understanding of the situation; Rita's version of it, that is. When she presently paused for breath, Coral, with the kindly intention of trying to reconcile the indignant newcomer to Camberside, ventured a bit of advice:

"Of course, it must seem frightfully hard lines to be penned up after a life like yours. Personally I'm glad I started school young, before I had time to think about running wild and all that; what you don't have, you don't miss. We're all sorry for you, of course, but if you'll take a word of warning from us, you'll stop your offensive against Miss Howard, whatever you think of her. Wait a minute!" here she waved down an attempt at fierce interruption from Rita. "Just let me finish the warning, there's a sport; I'm not presuming to dictate; I've seen and heard enough of you already to know it wouldn't be the slightest use, but *do* listen to this for your own sake. If you behave too aggressively to Miss Howard, it's bound to be noticed, even if she doesn't complain of you; you'll have the Head on your track in no time which will mean, as likely as not, that you would be cleared out, sent home you know; well! what would your grandfather do about your horse then, do you suppose? I bet he'd take Tommy away if you were packed off from here in disgrace."

Rita nodded grimly.

"You'd win the bet, there's not the least shadow of doubt about that. I think it's champion the way you and the others have listened to my ravings, and I'm not going to rail about any of you, however much I hate school itself; and thanks for the advice, which I'm going to take, in a way."

"In a way!"

The others eyed her speculatively, wondering just what was behind that sinisterly spoken addition, what plot of deepest dye was already hatched in the brain of the fascinating but fiery new girl. Not for long, however, did she leave them conjecturing. With a vindictive glint in her narrowed eyes and malicious nods of her bright head, she said hardly:

"I'm going to start a vendetta against the Howard creature. I'm here against my will, all through her machinations, and she shall pay for it. I'll dog her doings and harry her till she either leaves the school on her own, or is caught out, or driven into something that gets her dismissed. She won't be able to fasten on to me for aggressiveness because I'll not give her the chance. There's more than one way of persecuting people. I shall be subtle, subtle as—as—Satan!"

To say that shocked faces greeted this drastic announcement would be to put the listening girls on pedestals of virtue they would not righteously have graced. A modicum of awe was apparent here and there, but for the most part it was just honest-to-goodness interest that looked out of them. Anything that promised to endow term time with a bit of excitement, something about which to gossip other than the usual well worn topics, would be relished. Rita immediately sensed that, even when a peace lover feebly began the remonstrance she felt she ought to make in the name of the school and authority,

"Oh, but I say, Rita, I wouldn't——"

"Perhaps you wouldn't," Rita shut her up promptly. "You are not up against things as I am. So don't you say anything. I don't want one more word from you or anybody about what I shall or shall not do. My mind is made up. I'm going to make every day of the Howard's life a misery to her."

"You'll be done there, Terror," chuckled Coral.

"Done, eh?" came the sneering challenge. "Perhaps you'll tell me how."

Coral's grin was mocking.

"Certainly, anything to oblige. Your vendetta will have to be a Monday to Friday affair. Miss Howard goes home for week-ends."

"Home! Where? Why?"

"Categorically," informed Coral; "Yes, *home!* At Burlton, our nearest town, ten miles from here. Because her mother lives there, I suppose; anyhow 'Juppy' (Miss Jupp the Head, you know) lets her off on Friday evening till Monday morning."

Rita, bent on finding fault wherever Miss Howard was concerned, gave a disgusted snort.

"Well, I do call that cool," she cried. "She gets off to enjoy her week-ends of freedom, while the other mistresses are tied here to keep order."

Coral laughed good-temperedly.

"Oh, they don't have such a bad time of it.

There's no reason why Miss Howard shouldn't have her week-ends if it suits her and 'Juppy' to arrange the matter so; we're a pretty quiet lot on the whole."

"Yes! Deadly, I should say," was Rita's dry response to that. "School routine is enough to make anybody as dull as ditchwater, of course; that's why I so loathe the idea of it. Stagnation! that's what it amounts to. Well! Miss Howard was instrumental in getting me here, so she'll just have to put up with the consequences; I daresay I shall be able to get in quite a lot in the way of aggravation between Mondays and Fridays, and the week-ends will give me time to think up some more. I don't mean to stagnate, and I expect I shall stir all of you up before I've done. Camberside isn't going to be peaceful with me in it, I can tell you, especially while Miss Howard is in it, too."

Coral gave a careless shrug.

"Oh, well, if you're bent on making trouble, I suppose it will be waste of breath trying to talk you out of it. But watch your step, that's all. As to stirring us up, that remains to be seen. None of us would object to a few more

94

capers, but whether we get dragged into them depends upon the shape they take. If you really are the revolutionary you seem to be, we may find it safer to sit tight and be just lookers on at them. What say you, girls?" and she appealed to her friends.

They said it with one voice, in a general "Hear, hear!" backing up her strictly non-committal attitude.

But Rita simply snapped her fingers at the whole party and looked her defiance.

"There will be *no* sitting on the fence in *my* campaigns," she decreed flatly. "Girls who don't hold with my doings will jolly well have to make themselves scarce."

Coral took her up quickly. "Hi! hi! you must shake down a bit, my dear Pepperpot. Don't forget that we've all been at Camberside longer than you have. You can't expect us to alter our ways just to suit yours. Be reasonable, please."

"There's no reasonableness in her at present," Hilary put in jocularly. "But perhaps contact with us will instil a little in time."

Rita's aggressive expression gave place to a

grin; she had reached the school prepared to hate everybody on sight, but she found the breezy good-nature of the girls too disarming for that; at any rate, she felt that whether they eventually proved for or against her, she would hardly be able to quench a sneaking liking for them. That fact, however, must not be permitted to weaken her fight against school life; the big streak of contrariness in her bade her to guard zealously against that. With the thought in her mind, her eyes held a fiery sparkle in spite of her smile, as she retorted:

"Don't build up any hopes. I *never* take my pattern from other people."

Several of her listeners laughed outright at that, and Hilary fenced back with:

"I can believe that! You're probably like model hats and gowns are supposed to be—quite unique in their way. So it's quite on the cards that we may become copies of *you*."

"Which Heaven forbid!" breathed Coral, fervently. "I'm sure we shouldn't like to think of poor old Camberside being given over to a pack of rebels."

Rita regarded Coral speculatively. Of the

group present, she was the one who most appealed to the newcomer. She was a girl whose good looks were those of character. No mere doll-like prettiness was hers. Her eyes crinkled when she laughed, showing her good-temper, but she had a firm mouth and chin for all that. Not the sort to enter into a scheme unless she chose, but a good backer-up when she did, Rita decided, and determined that she must make a bid for Coral's comradeship in the near future.

"You've a law-and-order complex, I expect," she remarked, including all the girls in a kind of amused tolerance; "and, of course, girls who like school quite naturally try to stand by it; we all stick up for the things we like, although, personally, I'm at a loss to understand how *anyone* can enjoy the cut-and-dried, herd existence of a school. Still, we can't all think the same way, though I certainly *do* hope to rope you girls into my scheme of things. I bet I'll find the difficulty with most of you is just a love of jogtrot comfort; you're chary of kicking up your heels for fear of the lash of some kind of punishment afterwards."

Rita had kept the same air of cynical amusement through this diatribe, but her tone of raillery and her mocking glances at her listeners made most of them squirm; conscious of that, she waited interestedly for comments.

The first came from Coral, level-headed, as might be expected from a girl of her calibre.

"Well," she said, in a slightly drawling tone, "I don't say that you're not right there. Comfort is worth having, and a bit of wholesome fear isn't a bad thing, when it keeps the law and order you sneer at."

"And after all, Miss Firebrand," Hilary put in, "you don't allow horses to be unmanageable, do you? A colt has to be broken in."

Rita's eyes danced. Here was a topic after her own heart.

"Very neat little arguments," she said crisply, and nodding brightly at the last speaker. "Yes, colts have to be broken *in*, as you say, but not broken—there's a difference. A good and well-trained horse keeps his spirit; spirit enough to play up sometimes and get his own way; though I'll admit he's generally punished for it."

"There you are!" cried Coral triumphantly.

"Then he might just as well have behaved himself and escaped the licking or whatever he gets."

But Rita laughed her to scorn.

"*What* a dull life!" she retorted. "To lose the fun and thrill of a good old kick-up just for fear of the consequences! That isn't like a spirited horse, and it isn't like *me*. I've been sent here bang against my will, so I'm going to play up."

And with that arrogance and the sounding of a bell, there ended as strange a discussion with a new girl as could well be imagined.

CHAPTER V

VENDETTA

IN the happiest of circumstances it would have been impossible for a girl of Rita's whirlwind character to have been domiciled at Camberside without creating something of an upheaval among the other pupils. She afforded unlimited food for gossip and speculation with her good looks, her changing moods and her relentless animosity towards the English mistress. Within a few days of her arrival, she realized herself the centre of interest in the school, quite friendly interest, too, on the whole; and this in spite of her arrogant manner and outspoken distaste of her surroundings. This was really a matter for regret, because a lack of attention to her unbridled sayings and doings might have toned down her egotism and even have acted as a check upon her resentful impulses.

Accustomed to occupying the centre of the stage in her home surroundings, she took the limelight shed upon her at Camberside quite as a matter of course, and played the part she had set for herself accordingly. Therefore Miss Howard's secret hope that she would find her right level at school was doomed to disappointment from the outset. Without any desire to spy upon the girl, she felt in duty bound to adopt a somewhat watchful attitude towards her, having promised Mr. and Mrs. Conway an early report upon the way their daughter was reacting to school life, after the decidedly unpromising departure for it. So, as the days passed, she noted with increasing uneasiness the tendency of the other girls to be swayed by Rita's untamed ways, a degeneration in the conduct of the Fourth Form in particular giving her real anxiety.

She was almost driven to wish she had never taken the rustic holiday which had brought her into contact with the Conways. It had given her a much-needed rest and change at a minimum of expense, all of which had mattered tremendously, nobody outside her own family knew *how* tremendously; but if the benefit derived was going to be discounted by the worry of having introduced an undesirable pupil into the school, the holiday would not have been worth while. So Miss Howard told herself at times, but again at others, conscience accused her of being easily disheartened, cowardly. The very idea, it said to her, of allowing herself ever to dream that a girl of fourteen could seriously disturb the morale of a whole school. It was absurd! it was unthinkable. Besides, as if proper discipline could not bring the most difficult girl to order, in due time. Really, what had happened so far was only what she herself had anticipated. Rita was having a vogue; her unusual prettiness and virile personality had temporarily caught on. She had what sentiment-loving schoolgirls call a film face, and must of necessity, therefore, attract a good deal of notice, plus flattery, until followers either found someone or something else to enthuse about or grew tired of the temperamental young beauty. As a discerning mistress, Miss Howard was well aware of the fickleness of schoolgirls, and in this instance she tried to take fresh heart from the knowledge, although there were sometimes instances of transferred allegiance, which angered her, because of their supreme disregard for hurt feelings. She could not imagine any great sensitiveness existing in the imperious Rita, however, the girl was too self-sufficient altogether; in fact, a bit of neglect in the form of less notice would be a wholesome corrective.

But at the end of a month there was no sign of such a corrective being administered; instead, Rita's hold upon the imaginations of her schoolfellows appeared more firmly established, even the more steady of the girls finding it difficult not to be drawn into her insidious campaign against rules and regulations in general, and Miss Howard in particular.

That last, was where the cunning of Rita's schemes came in. All the actual aggravation fell to Miss Howard's lot, yet so little was allowed to be blatant enough for her to fasten upon; her patience was tried in a hundred little ways that she knew for subtle persecution, but only rarely could she make a case for punishment. Consequently, her nerves began to suffer; she grew conscious of a vague sense of irritation that prevented her from sleeping properly, and sent her about her duties in an exasperated frame of mind which found vent in fits of temper with her pupils. She began to get into a state of actual dread of class time; she seemed to be able to feel the tigerish gloating with which Rita's gaze followed her on every possible occasion, and she realized that she was losing grip on herself, that the unfriendly atmosphere was having a psychological effect upon her. And things that nobody in the school could suspect or or ever dream of, depended on her keeping her position. Half frantically, during her tortured hours of sleeplessness at night, she told herself that she must pull herself together, must not have a breakdown, knowing all the time that she was labouring under another strain, outside the life at Camberside, which was sufficient tax without the vexations being experienced there. What made matters worse, too, was that she occupied a decidedly lonely place in the school. For one thing, her week-ends at her own home took her away from the more leisured time there, when opportunities of friendly communing together offered themselves to the mistresses. But there again!

perhaps she would not have taken those chances if she could have done. Her attitude towards her fellow teachers was an aloof one that might have puzzled them, if they had come more into contact with her. She struck them as being very reserved, neither giving confidences nor asking any, and they left it at that, contenting themselves with a periodical inquiry of her mother, who, Miss Jupp had explained to them, was widowed and delicate.

So, all things considered, life for Miss Howard at this juncture was far from smooth. She could be under no misapprehension as to whom was directed the spirit of antagonism that Rita had awakened and was fostering in the school. She alone was the target for its barbed shafts.

Everything seemed to be going on in much the usual way between the girls and the other mistresses. Miss Howard heard no complaints, even of Rita, the opinion of her colleagues being merely that the new girl was a hoydenish specimen who was proving rather a handful at the moment, but who would eventually tame down and probably turn out to be a worker of more than average ability.

Yes, Miss Howard had to admit to herself at last that there was a definite campaign against her personally, and that in its very insidiousness lay its greatest chance of success. How could she go to Miss Jupp with a tale of undermined authority, when no other mistress had any serious complaint to make. Of what use to say that the behaviour of the girls was upsetting her nerves, when she could not even name a definite line of misconduct.

The trouble was more in the nature of a mental baiting. The girl was tantalizing in dozens of different ways. It was just a constant pin-pricking that went on. But if she were to report such a thing as that to the iron-nerved and placid Headmistress, she would be told that she must be out of health, that she probably needed rest and had better give up her work for a spell. She might lose her post, for Miss Jupp could not afford to be sentimental about a mistress; anybody who was not highly efficient and a good disciplinarian would soon have to make room for a woman who did possess these qualities. So if she allowed the treatment of the girls to get the better of her, the only course was a voluntary resignation of her post, and that would mean . . . But when Miss Howard got so far with her weary thoughts, her lips would tighten, and she would firmly decide that she must live down the trouble, and hold on to her job at Camberside at all costs.

Buoyed up by that determination through one of the trying days that seemed to have permanently become her lot, she bethought herself of an inquiry letter of Mrs. Conway's, as yet unanswered, partly through press of work, and partly because she had been shirking what she feared might prove a passage-at-arms with Rita. But the letter had to be answered some time, and there was her promised report, too, which she had been putting off writing day by day.

Well, she would just have to be as diplomatic as possible for the sake of Rita's parents. Her communication should go off that very evening. She glanced at her watch, and hurried from her room. There would be just time to interview Rita, and get her letter written before the prep. bell rang.

At the tennis courts a few minutes later a cry went up for Rita Conway.

"Miss Howard wants to speak to you," was the message conveyed to her.

Rita scowlingly eyed the message bearer as though she were to blame for it.

"Bang in the middle of a game; she *would!*" came the stormy protest. "This is our free time; what right has she to come poking round, interfering with it? Why couldn't she have spoken to me before we came out?"

"Can't say," was the crisp response. "I only know she waylaid me to fetch you, and that she's waiting for you on a seat outside the museum. If it's a duel, Rita, you can call on me as a second," and the knowing Cambersidian ran off with a laugh, leaving Rita to fling down her racquet in a rage, and unwillingly obey the summons.

For, flagrant disobedience she had up to the present forced herself to avoid, for fear that it might lose her the cherished Tommy. She felt quite sure that Miss Howard would take the very first opportunity of bringing about such a dire punishment, to pay her out for the scene at home, and her uncompromising attitude at school.

In full expectation of some of the rasping fault-finding into which Miss Howard had lately been betrayed, she approached the mistress with an air as bored as she dared display openly. Miss Howard noticed, resented, but ignored it.

She had been doing some quick thinking during her brief wait for Rita, and it had resulted in a determination to make another bid for the girl's tolerance. It was a poor substitute for the confidence and affection she had once hoped to win from her, but it seemed the only chance of ever curbing, or influencing her. So, although she had a controversial matter to bring up, she opened the conversation with a smile, and a friendly tone.

"Do sit, Rita, won't you? It is lovely out here this warm evening. I won't keep you many minutes, but I had a letter from your mother a few days ago which I really must answer now I have a little time to spare. I want to catch this evening's post."

She paused, hoping for some relaxing in the

girl's face that would put things on an easier
footing between them. But Rita, sitting as
bidden, though perfectly stiff-backed, on the
very edge of the seat, and as far as possible
from the mistress, just looked coldly watchful,
and murmured evenly: "Yes, Miss Howard?"

That was all; but glance and tone plainly
conveyed hostility and suspicion, and realizing
this, the other immediately felt at a disadvantage.
However, she still clung to her purpose of
trying to promote peace.

"I suppose your mother is feeling anxious
or—or perhaps a trifle hurt, Rita," she resumed
carefully. "She wrote me because she hadn't
heard much from you, and wondered, naturally,
how——"

Into the rather tentative speech the girl
broke contemptuously.

"What does she expect me to write, about
school? There's nothing much to say. I've said
that I'm well, that I hoped all at home were
well, and Tommy's leg better."

"Oh, but, Rita! my dear! you know she wants
to hear more than that." Miss Howard's earnestness would have melted most girls. "Surely you

could send her a chatty little note sometimes telling her how you are getting along, about the school, and so on."

There was a cynical flicker in Rita's eyes as she argued. "She'd only be cross at what I wrote, and Daddy would stop my pocket money. I'm not the least interested in the school. I shouldn't mind if it blew up to-morrow, and took ev-en-me with it. You *see* it's no use writing home in that strain. I should only let myself in for nasty letters back, and it's too much trouble arguing on paper."

Miss Howard, smothering a burning desire to be reprimanding, struggled along mildly.

"But why should there be arguing? There needn't be if you would only be as jolly as I've seen you sometimes with the girls. Ah! what about them, Rita? If you don't care to write about the school itself, why not tell your mother about your new acquaintances."

A mirthless little laugh greeted this suggestion.

"Girls! Gracious, Miss Howard, Mummy's much too busy to be bothered with letters about other people's girls. She has three of her own, remember, and she evidently thinks we are a handful to have so jumped at a chance to pack one off out of her way."

The only thing was to let that heresy pass without comment, Miss Howard decided desperately, and she gamely made one more attempt to save the situation.

"Then games, Rita! Surely you can——"

Right across that effort went a calmly ruthless interruption.

"Mummy knows already that I'm not very keen on ordinary games; they're too tame. I play tennis and such like here, of course, because there's nothing better to do, but——"

Here a shrug testified to Rita's scorn. With a wearied gesture, Miss Howard rose from the seat, and her tone indicated waning patience as she said: "I am to understand then, Rita, that you do not intend to write home anything that will make your people think you are happy?"

The girl, nearly as tall as the woman she stood now to face squarely, replied with cool deliberation: "If you mean, am I going to pretend that I'm happy just to please Mummy and Daddy, Miss Howard. No! I'm not. I can just let them know I'm well, and that's all. I told them I shouldn't be happy, and I'm not happy."

The thin crust of Miss Howard's wrath broke at last.

"I can well believe that," she snapped, her face a flame with temper. "You never will be happy while you think only of getting your own wilful way, and thoroughly upsetting everyone who thwarts you. I think you must have some dreadful kink in your nature."

She broke off abruptly. Miss Jupp's rather magisterial voice had suddenly sounded in the near distance, and the glances of both the verbal contestants flashed round, to see her coming along the gravelled way with some visitors, evidently with the idea of showing them the school museum.

Hastily the disputing pair regarded each other again, and it would have been plain to an observer that neither wished to meet the sharp-eyed "Head" at the moment.

"If you've finished with me, Miss Howard," Rita began, momentarily hurried out of her calm by the policy of avoiding any clash with the head of the school.

Miss Howard did not stay even to nod.

Afraid of the notice that her agitated state would be bound to attract she walked quickly away and disappeared round a corner of the museum.

"A kink, have I," was Rita's satirical thought as she made off in another direction. "Well, if a kinky nature helps me to drive her away from Camberside, I'll do my best to cultivate it."

With the finish of the interrupted game, she was pressed by the friendly Coral and Hilary for an explanation of the summons, and after satisfying their curiosity, she added:

"As a matter of fact, I should begin to make the best of being here, if Miss Howard were out of the way. I know I'm only 'cutting off my nose to spite my face' as the saying goes, acting pig-headedly over a thing I can't alter. But I can't be anything but contrary while she is about. My people aren't on the spot to see me, so they can't pat themselves on the back and say, 'I told you so,' if I let myself get more chirpy."

"But you *are* more chirpy than when you came; you can't deny it," chuckled Coral. "Can she, Hil?"

"Not if she tells the truth," was the other girl's agreement.

Rita gave a genial smile at the triumphant pair.

"Oh! well," she responded. "You two, and all the other girls as well for that matter, have been jolly decent. I simply can't help liking you all, though I came here full of hate for everybody and everything. And I still detest school life, mind you. Nothing will ever alter that, but as I said just now, it's a case of making the best of it unless I can see a way out. I must confess I can't, short of running away, that is."

"Where could you run *to?*" Hilary inquired blandly.

"Ah! that's where the catch comes in," laughed Coral, bent on steering the discussion into a lighter channel. "A boy could get away with it by making for a seafaring life, but there's no chance of that sort for a girl, unless she could make herself up to look old enough to pass for a stewardess."

"Whoa! Coral, don't put ideas into her head," shrilled Hilary, eyeing Rita in half-comic alarm, to see how she reacted.

"Faugh! there's no need for you to worry," Rita retorted, in a disgusted tone, "I'd sooner stay here than wallow in a ship, looking after seasick people. Still, I've got to liven things up a bit if I'm not to get melancholy or desperate. Look here, you generally seem game to follow my lead; what about a trip to the town next half-hol', just we three and the chosen few, making seven in all, a nice little party?"

The "chosen few" constituted four other Fourth Form girls upon whom Rita had condescended to bestow her special patronage, mainly because they belonged to the more daring element in the school, and, therefore, were among those who most appealed to her. But although Coral and Hilary came into the same category of lively ones, they both looked dubious now.

"Out of bounds, don't forget," Coral hazarded. She was unwilling to upset Rita, the firebrand, but realized the necessity of a warning.

It was received with a contemptuous sniff and a stormy outbreak.

"I'm not likely to forget. Everything that is of any interest round here is out of bounds. But who cares? At any rate, *I* don't and I'm *going*—with anybody else who has pluck enough."

"All right! All right! don't get huffy with Hil and me," remonstrated Coral hastily. "Just give us time to think over the innovation, that's all. You rather took our breath away, you know. But"—here her eyes began to sparkle —"I suppose it *could* be managed—with care."

Hilary, too, began to register excitement.

"With *very* great care, disguising ourselves a bit and all that, eh what?" she cut in.

Rita regarded both girls favourably, nodding slowly as she said:

"Anything, anything, to keep me from bursting with boredom."

"Very well," this blithely from Carol. "Then let's hope the end will justify the means. We're often being told not to do evil that good may come, but every rule has its exception. We really shall have to camouflage ourselves somehow though, as Hil suggests. It would never do for us to be recognized. Miss Howard would be the biggest risk."

"Miss Howard!" echoed Rita surprisedly. Then recollection flashed upon her. "Why! of course, she week-ends in the town! I'd quite overlooked nasty little details for the moment; but that needn't bother us. You two are not members of the school dramatic society for nothing, surely?"

They grinned understanding of the hint, and Coral said:

"No! *we'll* manage. But to make quite sure of safety we'd better not roam about town too noticeably. What about a cinema show?"

It was Rita's turn for a grin, and a wide one at that.

"Great, so far as I'm concerned," she agreed. "I've only been to film shows just now and again, so I'd love it, you may be sure. Come along now, quickly, let's round up the others and make definite plans; then I must write a letter home."

Somebody else was writing to her home while the secret pow-wow of seven was proceeding.

It was Miss Howard who penned it, pausing
often to knit her brow and bite her lips as if she
found it a difficult one to indite. Slowly and
carefully when it was finished, she read it
through.

"*Dear Mrs. Conway,*

"*I would not let Rita's short letters be a source of
worry if I were you. The fact that she has never been
away from home before, except for holidays, would
probably tend to make her an indifferent correspondent.
And the days are so full at school, as you will know from
your own experience; I sometimes think that life for
schoolgirls is over-organized, that they would be all the
better for more time to themselves in which to develop
their individuality. But I'm afraid my personal ideas
are not likely to alter things in that respect.*

"*However, when I tell you that Rita is distinctly
'all the rage' at Camberside, you will be satisfied, I am
sure, that all is as well with her as could be expected after
her unwilling début. In fact, I think that the admiration
she is undoubtedly receiving from the other girls will do
more than anything else could, to settle her; we are all
apt to appreciate, and be happy, under flattering conditions, are we not? So please have no anxiety, dear Mrs.
Conway; just leave Rita to time and companionship.*

"*I do not hear any complaints from the other mistresses
regarding her studies, so assume that she is making satis-
factory progress in this direction. . . .*"

A few polite platitudes ended the letter, and
Miss Howard congratulated herself that she had

concocted just the diplomatic screed she had aimed at. "I daren't write actual untruths," ran her troubled thoughts, "but on the other hand I don't want to make mischief; it would only give Rita cause for a real grievance against me. She may be quite different when she has had time to settle down, and the discipline is bound to do her good. I think my letter is as tactful and as truthful as is possible in the circumstances. I hate the very idea of those nice Conways being distressed by knowing what their daughter is really like to me, at all events. She is a dreadful trial and yet, I can't bear to think of her being deprived of Tommy. She'll shake down presently and forget her vindictiveness against me; of course she will!" and on that consoling reflection Miss Howard dispatched her letter.

By the same post that evening went a carelessly scribbled note from Rita which said:

"*Dear Mummy,*

"*Miss Howard has an idea that you are fidgeting over my short letters, but of course she's only romancing. Whatever* should *there be to fidget about so long as you know I am well?*

"I hope you and all the rest are, too. I am glad Tommy's leg is better. Give him a pat from me.

"And can I have some more pocket-money, please, before Saturday?

"Urgently needed by

"Rita."

"Well?" Mrs. Conway inquired of her husband when he had perused the two letters next morning.

He smiled at her. "Evidently things are going quite as I've expected, my dear, so don't worry," he said. "Rita's getting into the swim and forgetting her woes to the extent of letting bygones be bygones. At any rate, that's how I translate. In the circumstances, send the baggage some more cash by all means; she's having to do some treating in return for her popularity, I expect," and with a relieved mind at the thought of dispersing domestic clouds, Mr. Conway strode off laughing.

But the twins, still feeling rather desolated at the departure of their elder brother and sister, found nothing to cheer them in the letters of either. Jimmy's were nearly as brief as Rita's and were mainly concerned with his and other boys' prowess at games.

"Nothing seems to happen *but* games at Jimmy's school," Poppy remarked after perusal of one of the disappointing screeds.

"Well, that's something, anyhow," Tessa said. "You'd think from Rita's letters that nothing *at all* happened at hers. If school is as dull as she makes it seem, then I hope we never have to go. We'll behave extra well so's to keep on with a governess."

"Um-m-m!" Poppy sounded doubtful. "But it's pretty dull here at lesson and walk time without Jimmy and Rita. We never knew what explosions there were going to be; they kept things lively."

"That's so," admitted Tessa. "Still, there's plenty to do around the farm when we're free. What does Rita do after lessons, I wonder? She doesn't say a word about games or anything."

"Well, she must do something, or what does she want so much pocket money for?" Poppy argued, her mind on the letter which appeared to have satisfied her father, at any rate. " 'Urgently needed,' she said. What for and why in such a hurry, I wonder? I do hope she isn't thinking of disappearing again."

Tessa looked horrified. "Gracious! don't breathe such a thing! We don't want everybody worried again by anything like that."

"You needn't glare at me so," was Poppy's half resentful reply. "I'm sure I don't want to worry anybody. I was only wondering if Rita meant to."

Tessa pondered a few moments, looking anxious, then her face cleared suddenly.

"I know! Let's write and ask her about things," she suggested hopefully. "I expect she'll write more to us, especially when she finds that we want to know about everything. We haven't sent her a letter on our own yet, you know."

So the twins set about their correspondence then and there, the joint effort, of which each penned a half, resulting in this epistle:

"*Dear Rita,*
"*We do so want to know what school is like and how you are really getting on at Camberside, so perhaps you will send us a letter all to ourselves, as there is nothing much in the ones you send to Mummy and Daddy. Is it as nasty at school as you thought it would be? What are the girls like? Are the lessons hard and do you have any real fun after them? What's the food like? Are the*

*other mistresses interfering things like Miss Howard?
Does she try to take it out of you for being rumbuschus
now she has got you there? What's the head like? Does
she know about your not wanting to go to her old school
and try to sit on you for it? What sort of games do you
play, if any? What have you spent all your pocket
money on already and what do you want more so soon
for? You aren't thinking of running away again, are
you? If so, please don't, it's too nasty for everybody
else and Grandpa has got all right, so it would be a pity,
to upset him again. Besides, the police and everybody
would be on your track and would soon find you unless
you died your hair and that would be an awful pity; or
went abroad, and you wouldn't have enough money for
that; you'd have to be a stowaway and be dirty for days
among rats and things and not have enough to eat; you'd
have to chew cargo and that might make you sick. So
we shouldn't if we were you. Daddy laughed at your
letter and told Mummy to send you the cash you wanted
by all means, but we're ankshus about it. Miss Howard
said you are all the rage at Camberside. Is that true or
did she mean just 'all rage' and nothing else. Daddy
thinks she really means poplar with all the girls and we
quite expect you are, but we would like to know for certain
and what you treat them to if you are, because if we
were ever poplar, we wouldn't be able to afford much,
being two of us. This is a frightful long letter, so you
write us a frightful long one, too, because if school is awful,
we want to behave and hang on to a governess. We might
as well be in the know, as Jimmy calls it, as you have
got to be there. Tell us about everything. Your loving
sisters,*

"The Twins."

Even if this effusion had reached Rita when she was in an ill-tempered mood, it must have amused her, but it arrived when she was feeling pleasurably excited over the contemplated outing, and she laughed so immoderately that several girls came racing to her cubicle to see if she were having hysterics.

After the laughter, however, came reflection. Her eyes narrowing, she read the letter through again, suspicion lurking in her heart. Had the twins been put up to writing by their mother? Was she hoping to get information from Rita through them? A scowl darkened the girl's face. But it soon cleared. Recollection of her mother's fair, open ways bade her dismiss the suspicion as groundless. But having harboured it, she was cautious, all the same. Her reply, left lying about by the careless twins, might be seen by other eyes than theirs. So Rita wrote:

"*Dear Kids,*

"*Jimmy always says I've got a long tongue, so you'll have to wait till it wags at home again for the answers to all your questions. School is a place where one thing after another seems to come quicker than it does anywhere else. Anyway, you can never call your soul your own for long enough to write more than quite short letters.*

125

Re cash. It sort of greases the wheels sometimes. You'll find out just what that means if you ever go to school yourselves. Cheerio, kids.

"Rita."

But the only cheer the twins derived from that letter was a conviction that, at any rate, no fresh runaway attempt was being contemplated at present by their sister.

CHAPTER VI

NIGHT PROWLERS

TWO evenings later, Rita's shining head was thrust unceremoniously into Coral's cubicle, whence came a low murmur of voices.

"Ha! I thought I should find you here too, Hil," she said in a satisfied tone. "I've got the extra money I wanted from home; it arrived by the evening post, so now we can go right ahead with our plans for Saturday."

Her hearers made congratulatory sounds, Coral adding, however:

"But it doesn't seem fair that you should be doing most of the paying out, Rita. We others must refund you a bit out of our next pocket money."

"You'll do nothing of the kind!" was Rita's firm reply. "Who proposed this trip, pray?"

"Well, you did, of course, but——"

"Right!" chipped in the new girl again. "And who have made themselves responsible for getting the necessary rigouts, grease paint and so on?"

"Oh well! if you are going to look at it in that light," Coral began again.

"I am! certainly I am!" was the vigorous interruption. "I expect to pay out for a bit of fun. That's nothing! but you and Hil are going to take risks arranging our disguises. And the other four are going to do the manipulating of the garments you borrow, so I reckon we shall all be quits."

"It's jolly of you to say so, anyhow," Hilary chimed in sociably, "but no faking ourselves up would get us to town and a picture show without your extra cash, so we'll all contribute a little as soon as we can. It's awfully generous of you, Rita, to lay out so liberally; let's hope the outing will be as exciting and enjoyable as we mean it to be."

"Hear! hear!" Rita was showing more animation than she had done since her arrival at Camberside. "When shall you do the burgling?"

Coral considered, "What's to-day? Thursday! H'm! it'll have to be at once, to-night, that is, so that the chosen few can decide to-morrow night how to fit everybody up."

"What time?" was Rita's next question as she looked at her watch.

It was Hilary who answered on this occasion.

"Oh! late; quite twelvish, don't you think Coral?"

"Better be," was the laconic agreement, "in case any of the 'powers' are tripping about the corridors after a pow-wow with 'Juppy'; she's a fairly late bird. Which reminds me that I'm not. I can't possibly keep awake till midnight, unless I'm doing something active."

"Then just turn in as usual at 'lights out' and have a good snooze," Rita advised. "I don't get to sleep at all early here, it's missing my riding, feeling so irritated and all that, I suppose; besides I read for quite a while, so you can rely on me to call you at the witching hour of twelve. Now I'll hop a'ong and take the good news to the chosen, while the coast's likely to be clear," and she slipped away to the next dormitory, leaving her two chief allies to talk over the details of their night raid on the dramatic society's "props."

"There are lots of clothes packed away in the dressing-room that aren't likely to be used again for ages, perhaps not in our time at all, so if the chosen do have to hack them about a little, it won't matter," Coral said complacently. "We daren't look too freakish, we should attract notice and that's the last thing we want to do. Getting the stuff is the only bother; we must have some plausible tale ready in case we're seen by anybody; now *what*, I wonder? We couldn't *both* pretend to be sleep-walking, for instance."

"One of us could, the other could be following the 'walker' to see she came to no harm," Hilary proposed with a giggle, and as no better excuse could be thought of to fit the case in the event of surprise, it was decided that the pretence should be acted upon as a precaution, during the negotiation of corridors and stairs on the way to the school concert hall.

"Though what about coming back?" Coral debated suddenly. "Sleepwalker and Co. carrying bundles of 'old clo,' you know. The tale would sound rather thin, methinks."

Hilary gurgled with laughter, "I should say so! We should just have to drop the bundles in the shadows and retrieve them later. Anybody meeting us would get such a start that details wouldn't be noticed, probably. Anyhow, we shall have to chance a bit, but it isn't at all likely that anyone besides us will be prowling after midnight. Let's hope the moon keeps busy, then we won't need to use our torches, if at all, except in the 'props' room itself."

"Mind, Hil," Coral blurted out after a thoughtful minute or so, "much as I like a lark I shouldn't have joined in this one at the suggestion of anybody but Rita. She's a funny tempered fish and just about as self-willed as she can be, but there's something one can't help liking about her, too; and I feel sorry for her; she reminds me of a wild thing in harness knowing it can't get free but hurting itself by kicking, all the same. You know what I mean, you've seen young horses being broken in."

Hilary nodded, "Yes! it's really rough on her that she was allowed to run wild for so long. I believe what she says will prove true. She'll never *like* school."

Coral agreed, adding however: "But she'll probably find it bearable if she has an occasional fling, like this Saturday one for instance. That's my idea in playing up to her. And she may get more tolerant of Miss Howard in time, too. This bear-baiting we're all doing is pretty awful, really, when you think of it. Miss Howard is a bit odd lately, don't you think? Funny about the eyes."

"And the temper!" this dryly from Hilary. "Still, we are all leading her a dance, as you say; perhaps it's too bad. But then Rita is leading all of us by the nose, so, what would you?" and Hilary finished with a careless shrug.

"Magnetic! that's it. That just describes her," Coral said decisively. "And at present she's pulling us all to perdition, but if she ever turns the other way, she'll just as easily make angels of us all. Well! it's me for bed now, and you had better go to roost too, or we won't be ready for to-night's bad deed."

Some time later, the two emissaries were facing, blinky-eyed, the still very wide awake Rita.

"Well! you do look a bedraggled pair," she cautiously chaffed, after having heard their plan of action. "The sleep-walking idea is excellent, only for Heaven's sake, stop those yawns, Coral. A sleepwalker wouldn't yawn, you know; and now, see here! I can't possibly sleep while you are on this rampage all through me, so d'you mind if I follow? Keeping my distance, of course, because three would be a crowd if we were seen, but I'd love to help to get out the clothes."

"Come by all means if you don't mind the risk." Coral told her. "But do be careful, Rita; you're not so sure of the passages and doors at that end of school as Hilary and I are. Don't blunder into a nest of seniors, it would be nearly as dangerous as falling foul of a mistress."

"Trust *me* to look out!" Rita said in her cock-sure way. "Go on, now! I'll give you five minutes start in case you have to do any pulling up and hiding."

Hilary was not the only one that night to follow what might have been a sleepwalker.

The restless Rita, creeping along through the silent building in dressing gown and slippers after having given the pyjama'd pair the pre-arranged start, only just smothered an amazed ejaculation when a familiar figure emerged from a corridor opposite the one she was traversing.

Miss Howard!

Rita held her breath and pressed herself flat against the wall of her corridor as the mistress, made visible to her by the moonlight shining through a big landing window, turned towards the staircase.

Edging herself along and peeping round her own corner of the corridor, Rita watched Miss Howard begin the descent, then urged by a somewhat awed curiosity, she followed, asking herself unanswerable questions as she did so.

What was Miss Howard thinking of, sneaking about the school fully dressed at this time of night? Where was she going? And why was she looking so peculiar? Rita had caught a glimpse of her face looking pale and preoccupied. Had she had any bad news? Or, horror! had Coral and Hilary been unlucky enough to make some noise which she was off to investigate. That fear quickened the pace of the tracker. But no! it couldn't be the girls she was after, Rita was soon assured of that, when Miss Howard crossed a wide lobby, unfastened a door at the back of the school and passed out into the moon-ridden night, closing the door softly after her.

Even more cautiously Rita turned its handle a few seconds later, peering through the merest chink until dead silence and solitude emboldened her to open it wide enough to thrust her head beyond the threshold. Then she, too, slipped out; she, too, shut the door from the outside; she, too, took the moon-dappled avenue to the school chapel, picked out by nature's flood-lighting on rising ground a couple of hundred yards or so away from the school itself.

On! on! went the lithe figure of the mistress, and on! on! went the equally lissom form of the follower.

"Thank Heaven," Rita communed with herself as she slunk along, careful to keep in the shadows, "that it's neither cold nor wet, or I might be sneezing an alarm before this little trip ends. Thank goodness, too, that we aren't in a main thoroughfare, where policemen might be patrolling; we'd look a mighty rum couple stealing along one after the other like this. Is she sleep-walking or what? La! la! but it's eerie!"

135

Her feeling of creepiness was subservient to her curiosity, however. Whatever she felt like, wherever the adventure took her, she meant to satisfy it regarding the nocturnal doings of the woman she detested. If sleep-walking proved to be the explanation, a hint of it reaching Juppy would surely mean that Miss Howard would have to resign her post; a mistress who did midnight rambles in her sleep wouldn't do at all; anybody would understand that. And if somnambulism *wasn't* causing this little gadabout, what was? What intrigue or crime of deepest dye, could be at the bottom of it? A person didn't sneak about at dead of night for nothing expecially when that person happened to be a supposedly highly-respectable mistress of a boarding-school.

Spurred on by these racing thoughts, the girl kept to her sleuthing, pausing only where the avenue finished, leaving a space of some thirty yards to be traversed to the Chapel door, with only one ancient yew tree about half way to afford a cover.

"I shall have to look out for myself now," was the tracker's uneasy thought as she watched her quarry. But as Miss Howard swerved slightly to the right on nearing the chapel door, Rita took a chance and halted pantingly a few seconds later, behind the yew's stout trunk. A minute or so after that she was saying to herself: "Dare I?" then, having dared, was soon holding her breath as she cautiously pushed open the door left ajar by the woman who had entered it just before her.

Moonshine glinted into the chapel, giving just sufficient light for Rita to creep into a back seat, and, crouching down, watch the other's proceedings from over its top; at least, while her dim figure could be seen, which was while she threaded the last part of her way towards the organ, then Rita's curiosity had to rely on her ears only. For Miss Howard vanished behind the curtain that hid its seat, and the tracker had to wait in a quivering suspense during a few minutes stillness broken by only the slightest of noises in the unseen region.

Conscious that any movement of her own might be heard now, Rita dared not attempt an advance, much as she longed to get a glimpse of Miss Howard's doings.

"Wonder if she's a spiritualist and has come here to hold a séance on her own?" Sudden shivers travelled down Rita's back at the idea, which she struggled to banish quickly, before dread should send her into a panic. Self control became a difficult matter all at once, however, as there flashed before her mental vision the harassed look Miss Howard's pale face had worn as she had been about to leave the school.

"Ugh! I'll get outside in case she starts trying to call up spirits. I believe I should scream if she did anything uncanny!" was Rita's sudden decision, and she was just about to essay a noiseless departure when a flood of soft sound arrested her movements.

Coral and Hilary exchanged surprised and rather uneasy glances presently, over their respective bundles of clothes, which they had purloined from the heterogeneous collection in the props' cupboard.

"Where can the tiresome creature be?" Coral murmured in a worried undertone. "There's light enough for her to have found her way along by this time, surely, even without her torch, which she's certain to be carrying for any dark part or emergency."

"H'm! pity she arranged to come after us, perhaps." Hilary looked a trifle strained as she spoke. "The fewer there are on a job of this sort, the better. She may be hung up somewhere, hiding on account of someone about, though who *should* be at this hour, goodness knows! We've been here quite a while choosing, the half hour struck some time ago, so it must be getting on for one o'clock. What shall we do? We can't stick here waiting now we're ready."

"No! Oh no!" Coral replied hurriedly. "We must get back. Perhaps we shall run into her on the way. If not and she comes here after we've left, she'll know where we are and follow us back, of course. So come along." She picked up her bundle but only to drop it again like a hot cake as faint scratching and tapping noises sounded. "Heavens, what's that! Quick!" and she snapped off her torch, Hilary following suit with hers instantly.

The noises continued, sending cold shivers down the girls' backs and their gaze flitting wildly around, coming to rest at last at one of the windows. Then, if terror hadn't struck them momentarily dumb, they would probably have roused the school with affrighted yells at the sight of a face peering in at them. But mercifully, before their tongues could loosen to their undoing the face pressed closer to the pane, showing an aurora of auburn ringlets, and they recognized Rita.

"Good gracious! What is she doing out there?"

With the words, Coral switched on her torch again and sprang for the window.

"At last!" breathed Rita, when she was safely inside. "Do you know, I couldn't be sure of the right window; tried lots before I found you; sorry I scared you, though, my goodness! you both looked absolutely terrified," and she melted into soft laughter.

"Small wonder, you wretch, startling us like that just when our nerves were all on edge already," Coral scolded. "Apart from our errand we were in a positive dither because you hadn't turned up. Where have you been? And what has been happening?"

The laughter died out of Rita's face; a sort of vindictive triumph reigned there instead.

"Ah! where indeed? What indeed?" was the tantalizing response, which she followed up dramatically with: "You shall know all, but not here! Back we trot for all we're worth if you're ready. We're not the *only* night ramblers in this establishment, let me tell you."

CHAPTER VII

OUT OF BOUNDS

"NOW! what's it all about? What have you been up to?"

The council of three, breathing freely again after a nerve-straining glide back to their dormitory, sat on Coral's bed.

"Tracking Miss Howard!" was the wholly unexpected answer.

"Tr—tr——" Hilary was beginning, when Coral surged in with vigour.

"For Heaven's sake go on quickly, Rita. Tracking her? Where? And whatever for? What was she doing?"

"Playing the organ," Rita said with exasperating dryness.

Her listeners looked incredulous.

"But, the organ! After midnight!" Coral exclaimed, "Why, in the world should she?"

Rita waggled her curls. "Ah! there you have me," she said, "though I don't mind venturing a guess that she's mad. She gave me a frightful scare, but I'm glad I kept my head enough to follow her."

"So are we! Tell on!" urged Hilary vivaciously; a mysterious tale told in the small hours of a morning made a special appeal to imagination.

"Was she sleepwalking, do you think?" Coral broke in to ask. When Rita had given a brief outline of her experience.

Rita puckered her brow in indecision. "I can't make up my mind whether she was sleepwalking or whether she has gone queer in the head. She was fully dressed and I don't know if sleepwalkers have ever been known to put their clothes on before perambulating; of course, she may have gone up late and dropped off to sleep reading or correcting. Anyhow, her face looked strange, I thought. I didn't see her eyes. Luckily for me, they seemed to be looking down as she walked. I expect mine were nearly bolting out of my head when I found she was off for a midnight ramble. Naturally I was relieved in a way; I knew then that she couldn't be after you two."

143

"It's a mercy she didn't look round and see you following if it wasn't sleepwalking," Coral said, "and I don't think it could have been. Surely nobody could play the organ while asleep, the touch of the keys and the sounds would awaken anyone, I should imagine. Still, as I've had no experience of sleepwalkers, it's impossible to be certain, as you say. Did she have any trouble in finding the key-nail, do you know?"

"Couldn't have had. I wasn't a minute behind her, and by the time I was lurking under the shadow of that old yew nearest the chapel door, she had the key in the lock; I distinctly heard it grate as she turned it."

"I didn't even know she could play the organ," was Hilary's next contribution to the discussion. "Still, she's a secretive sort; nobody knows much about her, anyway. What was her playing like? Good? and what sort of pieces did she play? Dreamy ones, I suppose?"

Rita chuckled. "Not a bit of it," she answered. "I'm not a scrap musical, but I *do* know that they wouldn't have suited Juppy for voluntaries. Lively sort of things that went with a swing mostly, but played awfully well at that. She sounded quite clever at it. One thing I noticed though; she kept everything very soft."

"Ah-h-h-h! Then I bet she was awake all right and merely being careful not to be heard, as she thought." This from Coral, with all the triumph of discovery.

"Sounds feasible," Rita conceded, adding: "If she were a musical genius or a composer I could understand her capering out to play at all hours as the spirit moved her, but there's nothing of that about it, I'm convinced. So I vote we just lie low and say nothing, except to the chosen, and see if she shows any other signs of being mental. A few items of this sort for Juppy's ear presently, ought to persuade her to dispense with Miss Howard's services at Camberside. A half mental person couldn't possibly be considered fit for schoolmistressing."

The other two girls regarded their companion in puzzled silence for a few moments. It seemed unthinkable to them that Miss Howard could be anything but sane; she had always appeared so completely normal, likeable too, until this upheaving sort of term. The only thing that inspired any doubt at all in them was the fact that she had been different of late, both in looks and disposition. But although they did sometimes feel a little conscience-stricken at playing her up so frequently at Rita's instigation, they could not seriously believe that a mistress would really worry herself over an outbreak of tiresomeness that might easily be accounted for by the fag of the summer term. No! the change in Miss Howard and this nocturnal stunt of hers savoured of mystery.

"I wonder you had the nerve to stay and listen all the time, if you thought she was mental. It must have seemed a bit eerie," Hilary said after the short pause.

"It did!" Rita admitted. "But I stuck it out because I wanted to make a closer inspection of her when she left the chapel. Forgetting everything but that, I slipped out and got under the yew tree again when she finished playing, consequently she was ahead of me again and I got locked out. Hence my agitated hunt for the 'props' room window. I was in a frightful funk lest you should have gone upstairs again. I saw myself smashing a pane in desperation and being hunted as a burglar. However, here we are, all safe and sound with the clothes, plus item number one 'The Midnight Musician,' against Miss Howard."

"Did you get a better view of her after all?" Coral inquired.

Rita got up, stretching wearily. "No! a cloud was partly over the moon just as she passed me. But I heard her, muttering like anything to herself. She's batty, I do believe. Heigh-ho! and I shall be batty too if I don't get some sleep. To bed, all of us! Good morning!"

But to Carol and Hilary sleep was an impossibility for quite a while after Rita was soundly off. Triumph at having so successfully shadowed her bête noir had put her into a good temper, and the walk in the cool night air had had a soothing effect, in spite of the excitement attending the ramble. Her two companions in intrigue, however, puzzled and genuinely disturbed by the events related, could not settle themselves, so kept up a whispered confab for a time in Carol's cubicle, which was between Hilary's little apartment and that occupied by Rita.

"How she could manage to drop off soundly like that within a few minutes after such a nerve-racking experience, beats me," was Hilary's rather rueful comment on Rita's present sleeping powers. "The whole affair has got me into a dither, wondering and wondering. It's pretty awful to think that Miss Howard might be off her head."

Coral looked perturbed, too, though she hastened to be reassuring.

"Oh, I can't think that. Of course, one does hear of people having nervous breakdowns and getting brain storms, but Miss Howard has always seemed so very normal; until lately, anyhow."

Hilary's slow nod was ruminative. "Yes, *until* lately, as you say. But that's just it. And we must ask ourselves the question seriously, I think. Is all the playing up getting her down?"

"Surely not," demurred Coral. "I've never known a mistress yet who turned a hair at troublesome pupils; not really, I mean, though they are all apt to get huffy at times, of course. There may be a dozen things worrying Miss Howard, about which *we* know nothing. Her home affairs, for instance. Her week-ends don't mean relaxation, perhaps, for some reason."

"H'm! that may be," Hilary admitted, "though I can't see why anything like that should set her gallivanting at night. One would think she'd only be too glad to rest while she could."

Coral pondered, remarking after a short pause: "Rita seemed to doubt it, but Miss Howard might be a composer, or be trying to become one. To me, that seems the most feasible explanation of her organ visit, apart from the sleep walking one; and that doesn't sound very likely in the circumstances."

"The question is, how are we to find out?" the other girl wanted to know. "Because we ought to solve the mystery," she added.

"Certainly," agreed Coral. "We can't have a lunatic at large, just supposing her to be one. We shall have to take turns watching out for her for a while."

"And tracking!" Hilary sounded none too keen on that.

Her companion shrugged. "Not a job we shall fight for, I bet," she said with a grin, "but it will have to be done if we're to find out anything. Just watching Miss Howard flit off and return won't tell us what's on."

"Perhaps Rita will take on the outside detective work," was Hilary's hopeful comment. "It needs good nerves, which she most evidently has, judging by her sleuthing to-night. She'll really relish the job, too, I expect; we'll ask her to-morrow."

"To-morrow?" echoed Coral, giving a prodigious yawn. "To-day, you mean! My good Hil, don't forget we're in the small hours of it already. Let's go to bed now; we must, or I shall be too dead tired even to see my breakfast."

And with that, the two weary-eyed whisperers repaired to what rest their surging speculations would allow them.

One o'clock on the Saturday found the seven venturers on the top of a bus which they had boarded at a quiet spot on the main road that ran through Burlton, a town of some size a quarter of a mile up a tidal river from the coast. The girls were transformed very effectually; the borrowed clothes had been skilfully adapted to make them look much older, and the clever use of grease paint and make-up by Coral and Hilary, two of the shining lights of Camberside's dramatic society, had quite altered everybody's appearance besides. The preparations, thoroughly rehearsed late the night before, had taken only about a quarter of an hour inside a small copse, not far from where they waited for the bus; the actual dressing consisted merely of slipping thin grown-up frocks of sorts over their summer garb, a change in their mode of hairdressing altering their appearance tremendously. So, with their tell-tale school hats tossed out of sight inside a hollow tree-trunk, to be retrieved on the return journey, they felt they could meet, with perfect confidence in their disguise, anybody who had seen them as Cambersidians.

Spirits soared higher and higher as the bus neared the town. The taboo on all places of amusement during term-time, made this unexpected chance of a cinema show all the more exciting.

"Of course, if you'd rather we spent the cash some other way, do say so," was Rita's

obliging offer when they had all alighted.
"Boating, for instance; the river looks jolly."

"Oh no, no! the show, please," her friends
chorused, Coral adding. "We're just as keen on
the films as you are."

"Good!" cried Rita, obviously pleased, "and
anyhow, there will be plenty of time for a rattling
good tea afterwards. Now which way do we
go?"

The picture-house was soon located, and the
girls had just crossed the street to its entrance
when Rita jerked out excitedly:

"Look, who's coming! Eyes left!" and each
pair of orbs was obediently focused just in
time to see Miss Howard bustle hastily forward
and turn in at a door of the picture palace. They
saw Rita glide forward unaccountably, too, stoop
for an instant, then straighten again.

The girls fairly goggled at each other.

"Couldn't have been her. She must have a
double!" exploded Hilary after a tense moment.

"But it was the Howard, our dearly beloved
Howard. Of course, it was!" insisted Rita.
"Fancy catching her at it! Oh ho! item number
two for Juppy's ears. What luck that we came!

And look! you saw her ratting in her bag; she dropped this. Come out of the way a minute and we'll see what it is."

The scrap of paper which Rita had seen fluttering unheeded from Miss Howard's possession, proved to be a short note which had been sealed but now spread half open to curious eyes.

"Saturday.

"Dear Grace,

"Five o'clock will be a safe time for you to get to the island to-day and below is my list of requirements. If you should see red, keep off till you don't. I will have the coast clear for you as near the time mentioned as possible, but you know how things are with me sometimes.

"Your hermit Jack."

"Did you *ever!*"

One of a huddle in a secluded corner, Coral looked round at the rest in helpless amazement. Heads were shaken as helplessly; nobody else seemed capable of speech at the moment, but with recovered breath, Rita said:

"She's a thorough dark horse! That's my opinion."

"A madwoman perhaps, as you thought," Hilary hazarded. "This island that's mentioned may be a lunatic colony or something that she's escaped from."

Everybody stayed silent long enough to digest that possibility, then Coral came out with,

"Well! I don't know; we're up against a thumping problem by the look of it, and the only way to solve it is to shadow the creature who has set it."

"Hurrah! my sentiments exactly," applauded Rita. "Let's get along inside; there's the show to see and perhaps we shall get a sight of her, when the lights go up."

But there was no sign of Miss Howard anywhere within the range of her quizzing pupils, and they had just come to a whispered agreement to hurry out quickly and watch for her in good time, when they were treated to a sight of more interest to them just then than any picture. For up from the depths in front of the stage sounded an organ and seated at it was—Miss Howard!

Rita said afterwards that the show itself on that afternoon was absolutely wasted on her and her companions but that they had their money's worth, all the same, in brain exercise.

For speculation positively ran riot upon the strange doings of Miss Howard. That a woman who was regarded by Cambersidians as definitely a "highbrow," one who held decidedly scornful views of picture-houses, should descend to giving musical performances in one, was almost incredible.

The girls would never have believed such a thing possible had they not seen it for themselves. The surreptitious practice on the chapel organ was explained, but, the cheek of it! And this, of course, was why the English mistress wanted her week-ends in Burlton. Perhaps the story of her keeping a widowed mother company was all a myth. About the island, too? What island? Where? And who was her hermit Jack whose letter read so mysteriously, sinisterly, even?

"Phew! I couldn't have stayed in the stuffiness much longer; my head is a perfect whirl with puzzlement," murmured Rita later, when all seven of the girls had emerged in a rush from the building, to watch for their quarry. "For Heaven's sake don't look too goggle-eyed," she went on urgently; "we don't want to be taken for lunatics. Just look careless, but melt after her when she appears."

The melting involved a "dodging-the-traffic" game, during which the band kept together by a miracle, and ultimately a wild scramble for a bus top from which necks were craned and bulging eyes watched for Miss Howard, who was downstairs, to alight.

The river shore was their next objective, and from there, seated like a party of picnickers, they saw the extraordinary Miss Howard push off in a laden boat from what was evidently a private landing stage, and row easily down-stream on an outgoing tide.

CHAPTER VIII

ON THE TRACK

"A BOAT! a boat! My kingdom for a boat!" Hilary groaned as the seven watched their departing quarry.

"Kingdom be bothered! It's our teas that will have to be sacrificed," Rita said practically. "That is, of course, if every one is willing to forego the 'tucking' for the sake of the tracking?"

"Goodness, yes! If you mean hiring a boat. We can't give up the chase now. Who knows what desperate work we may be meant to expose!" was Coral's energetic backing, and the series of willing assents further clinched the matter.

"Good comrades!" Rita praised. "We'll try to scrape up enough for a cup and a cake later, and make up for such sparse fare another time. I vote we bolt for that boat-house farther along; disguised though we are, we don't want to risk attracting attention by pushing off from the immediate neighbourhood. Besides, do you see that bungalow lying back a bit, though right in line with the landing stage? It might be her home, and we *might* look suspicious to anyone peeping out." The cautionary measure was considered good, so the seven sprinted their hardest along a path behind the bushes that bordered the sandy shore, able to keep Miss Howard well in view meanwhile.

Negotiations for the hire of a boat were carried through without any trouble, the girls' skilful handling of the craft soon furnishing any evidence that was needed, of their right to be trusted with it.

"Goodness only knows what we're letting ourselves in for," Coral remarked, as their boat swung down the river after the one now being wave-tossed by the more boisterous water at its mouth.

"If we're late back at school we look like having such a tale to tell," broke in Rita, "that lateness won't matter in the least."

Coral laughed. "But you forget, Rita, what any tale we might have to tell would involve.

It would mean letting the cat out of the bag absolutely; we should have to tell Juppy where we had been."

"Well!" drawled Rita. "And what of it? Surely a free pardon for a mere breaking of bounds ought to follow our unmasking of an adventuress!"

"Humph! We've got to prove Miss Howard is one before we talk about unmasking her," Coral retorted.

"But what else *can* she be unless a lunatic, as I've mooted before? I ask you?" argued Rita.

However, increased vigilance demanded by the chase now put a stop to the wordy fencing, all attention having to be given to Miss Howard's movements and the necessity of not giving her any inkling that she was being followed.

Pulling strongly, she headed her boat out to sea, bearing towards the right, however, as soon as she had cleared a towering headland. This manœuvre soon gave the girls an opportunity of putting on a spurt, because the great thrusting cliffs hid her for some minutes; not until the girls themselves had breasted the point could they see that she was making for what was evidently a rocky islet about half a mile distant from the mainland.

The girls who were rowing rested their oars and everybody stared dumbly for a few moments.

At length: "What about it now?" queried Hilary with a suspicion of dubiety in her tone. And she added after the briefest of pauses, "If we follow her all that way we're almost sure to be late home."

Rita dipped her oar again significantly. "Can't help that; we've got to go on," she said doggedly. "I'm wondering now if she's in league with modern smugglers."

"Gracious!" shrilled one of the chosen. "Still! It's a perfectly possible solution of the mystery."

The idea gained ground quickly, Coral contributing.

"It certainly is. The cinema job suggests 'hard-up-ness' I should say, so it's quite likely that she is trying money-making in other directions, too. Anyhow, we can't hang back now, as Rita says. If we're late at all, it won't matter much how late; we may as well be hung for a sheep as a lamb."

So the chase was resumed, and with a seriousness that bespoke deadly earnestness.

As those that were merely a pleasure party out for a row, they presently sculled in leisurely fashion in the vicinity of what appeared to be a small natural harbour on the islet. They had watched Miss Howard's boat making towards it and disappear behind a jutting crag. Cautiously, then, they pulled closer and closer, their curiosity deepening when they were near enough to discern that what had looked at a distance like an oblong white speck, was really a notice board wired on to a spur of rock. Its message was in red lettering and ran as follows:

This island is private property. No pleasure parties allowed to land. Trespassers will be prosecuted.

"Ho! Ho! I dare say!" was Rita's ironical murmur for the edification of her friends. "Well! we're going to trespass, at any rate, and perhaps we shall be responsible for a prosecution. But it will never do to try landing here, of course. Let's row lazily along as if we're just taking an idle squint, and look out for a possible mooring."

Keeping as close into the lee of the little island

as was safe, they were well out of range of the orthodox landing place before they found a spot where they might attempt to get ashore. It proved a difficult and decidedly risky business, but at length the last girl scrambled on to a low mass of seaweedy rock and the boat was most carefully moored by a rope both fore and aft, so that there should be no fear of it breaking away and drifting.

"We can't afford to run the slightest risk of being marooned," Coral said, in a cautious undertone. "I only wish we could have hidden the boat; it's a bit conspicuous here, being a low part of the island," and as she spoke, her gaze swept searchingly the high craggy reaches that gave the islet a grim forbidding look, and from which many sinister eyes might be watching the intruders for all they knew.

That uneasy thought was in all their minds as they turned their backs on their one frail link with the mainland; nevertheless, not a girl hesitated, and even when the real climbing commenced, not one hung back.

With dogged persistence they scaled the succession of sharp and slippery rocks, silent except for occasional half-smothered exclamations over bumps and scratches and keeping together as far as the uneven mode of progress permitted.

So, precedence in the matter of arrival on a sort of rugged plateau high above sea level, was only a thing of seconds.

Rather winded by the strenuous climb, the girls clustered into an enthralled group, for the eminence was awe-inspiring, lofty enough to show the complete isolation of the great rock formation, as also its dark wildness.

Rita shivered suddenly. To a girl accustomed to the smiling countryside and the friendly sounds of animals and birds, the stark barrenness of the place and the sullen thunder of the waves seemed sombre and depressing.

"Quick!" she urged. "On with the exploring or I shall get the creeps! Ugh! it's a weird spot."

Her mood infected the others; readily enough the move was made.

The girls had been picking a way over the rough surface only a few minutes when the hum of voices, apparently floating up from the ground, pulled them all up sharply.

With a finger to her lips Rita enjoined absolute silence, then, after listening intently, she dropped on hands and knees and crawled on a few paces, peering all round at the rocky floor; success evidently rewarding her survey, she suddenly turned an excited face to her friends and beckoned them after her.

What she had found was a narrow fissure through which the voices came up, apparently from a cave below, and while their gaze travelled onwards to a cliff-like edge that doubtless overhung the cave opening, the ears of the girls were strained to make out something intelligible from the muffled murmur of sounds.

They were foiled, however; not a single word of the conversation could they catch; the only distinguishable fact was that it was carried on by a man's deep rumble and a woman's softer tones, Miss Howard's, they presumed.

Fearful lest the speakers should make an appearance and discover them, the girls looked desperately around for a hiding place.

"S-S-S!" Rita hissed suddenly and no sooner had her pointing finger indicated a semi-circle of rock than a scurry was made for it.

Over this roughly serrated barrier, which was almost on the edge of the rocky precipice, they could peer over with little risk of being discovered, so long as necks were not craned out too far.

It was a job to keep necks within bounds a few minutes later, when, into sight from a winding narrow track some thirty feet below, there appeared Camberside's intriguing English mistress being armed down the rugged path by a tall young man.

"Going back, I bet," Coral muttered, *à propos* Miss Howard, and nudging Rita. The latter agreed. "Now's our chance to get lower and try to explore; but we must be cautious in case there's somebody else below. Probably that man is seeing her to the boat. Hustle, everybody! If there is a cave, we shall probably find out all we want to know in a brace of shakes."

But it was soon plain to the girls that a considerable détour would have to be made; an overhang of rock prevented any descent from where they were.

During their hunt for a way down, they presently got a glimpse of the little rocky cove

165

where Miss Howard's boat awaited her, and as they looked, she and her mysterious cavalier appeared beside it, evidently still deep in an earnest confab.

"Can anybody make anything of it?" Coral inquired as they all stopped involuntarily to gaze for a minute or two, as though eyes might glean information denied to ears.

Most of the heads were shaken, but after a moment Hilary remarked thoughtfully:

"Well, Miss Howard evidently isn't taking anything away, so it can't be smuggling, can it?"

"Unless she's doing the smuggling! She came with a load, remember."

All eyes switched surprisedly on Rita and somebody asked her:

"Yes, but what should she smuggle and why?"

"Anything and everything that might be needed here by an escaped convict," came the startling reply. "It's an idea, anyhow."

It certainly was! And the more the girls thought of it, the more possible it seemed. Not that they wanted to put the young man down as a criminal; it was horrid even to think such a thing; he had looked quite attractive and quite respectable, so far as they had been able to see. But of course, attractive and respectable looking men were sometimes rogues; or, again, there was such a thing as a quite innocent person being wrongly convicted. Somebody mooted that aloud, and schoolgirl warm-heartedness immediately fastened upon the charitable suggestion.

"That's about it, if he is a convict," Hilary said, obviously in great haste to believe the best of him.

"Was," corrected one of her colleagues. "He doesn't look a bit like one now; didn't you notice what nice hair he had, for one thing?"

"Goodness! hair soon grows," was Coral's bland interruption, "and if he is, or rather was, a convict, the growing of a good head of hair would be his first care after escape, I should say. And he would have every chance, in a solitude like this."

"But I don't see how we're to know. He would be sure to have destroyed any incriminating signs of what he had been—convict clothes, bottles of hair restorer and so on"; this little summing up came from Hilary.

Rita burst into a laugh. "Oh, I say!" she cried. "Don't take my escaped convict idea too literally, or you won't be able to keep an open mind on the matter. I don't want you all suddenly developing the conviction that he's a murderer at large or something else awful, or you'll all be racing off in a blue funk at any minute."

"Keep calm!" Coral chuckled. "We're all far too curious to do anything of the kind, I'm sure, whatever bees we get in our bonnets. And after all, we're quite a party; even a desperate character, if the man proved one and we fell foul of him, would find us a problem to tackle *en masse*."

"That's so," Rita agreed cheerfully, quite assured regarding the nerve of her followers. "Still, we don't want to fall foul of him yet, or we won't find anything out, perhaps. Let's get on again quickly, just keeping a weather eye on our plotters whenever we can."

So the search was continued at once, after a last long look at the two figures still standing together on the shore by the cove.

Another vista in that direction a little later

showed Miss Howard afloat again, pulling back to the mainland. But what the girls could not see was the tall young man, with angry puzzlement in his eyes, bounding from rock to rock with the sureness of a mountain goat towards their boat.

After extensive manœuvring of rather dangerous situations and a poking and peering into darksome holes, an electrifying pronouncement went up from Rita.

"This is it! this is it! A positive little home from home, by the look of it, too."

The other girls rushed with headlong haste to the gap in the rock-face out of which she had thrust her head and was beckoning imperatively.

A sudden idea took Coral a step back to look upwards, and pointing after a hasty scanning.

"Yes! there's the sort of rock wall we were peeping over. You're right, Rita!" Then she crowded through the opening with the rest to stand wide-eyed on the threshold of a huge cavern flooded with electric light. But the illumination was not to be seen from outside. The opening appeared only like a big recess with a solid rock back, till a few steps inside to right or left showed it a passage-way into the cave, the rock back of the passage forming a kind of massive supporting pillar.

Rita rubbed her eyes, then turned them amazedly on her companions.

"Are we in a dream or is it an Arabian Nights Entertainment?" she inquired of them in a tone of almost comical wonderment.

Hilary sniggered nervously. "We won't find it either a dream or an entertainment if a modern smuggler or some other desperado comes and catches us here," she reminded.

But inquisitiveness had Rita firmly in its grip; to talk to her of the need for caution was useless.

"We'll chance it," she said, adding as her roving glance went everywhere: "There's an inner cavern! Look! Over to the right! I expect we shall find a positive warren of them. Quickly! Let's explore the extent first and quiz more carefully if we've time. There's plenty of room to dodge anybody in this big cave, but we might be rather boxed up in smaller ones."

It was an eerie thought, and it dominated strongly the girls who were of a more timid nature. So, one rather shrinking glance around the inner rock apartment was enough for their fearful souls, they dallied uneasily near the entrance; Rita's stare around was boldness itself, however.

"The place looks as though the black arts might be practised in it," she averred, "but even so, if the devil himself appears, I'll see all there is to see now that I'm here; you others can vamoose if you like."

"We'll do nothing of the kind," Coral stoutly declared, with a meaning look at the nervous ones. "A few shivers down the spine aren't going to drive us out till we've done the spying we came for."

"A brave speech, I suppose you think, but I consider it infernal impudence."

With startled gasps, the interlopers spun round to confront, not the devil, certainly, but a man in a devilish temper, to judge by his harshly spoken words and furious face.

"What the deuce are all you sneaking cats doing in here?" he demanded hotly.

Rita's blood was up in an instant. Cool reasoned questioning might have shamed her, but she met temper with temper.

"Just trying to find out what somebody just as sneaky is up to and we're going to find out before we budge. So don't you dare to shout at us!" she flared.

"Dare! Dare!" the man roared, shaking clenched fists. "You to talk of daring! How dared a pack of prying, meddling females land on my island, for one thing! You'll dare to tell me that you didn't see my notice to trespassers, I suppose?"

"Nothing of the kind!" fumed Rita. "We did see it, and it made us all the more keen on landing, to see what was going on here, especially as we——"

She checked her tongue just in time; it might be disastrous to say that they had seen Miss Howard land on the island. The man would naturally wonder more who they were. He might connect them with Camberside in spite of their present unlikeness to schoolgirls.

He was eyeing them narrowly now, fairly bristling with suspicion, and, as if he sensed the uneasiness his searching glare occasioned in the girls, a sneering smile curved his lips.

"Especially as you, what?" he taunted.

172

"Something better left unsaid, eh? Something better hidden, eh?" As the last cynical utterance left his mouth, he made a sudden spring at the girl nearest to him and before any of the half petrified lookers-on could make a move, he had whisked out a handkerchief and was rubbing his victim's face hard, giving merciless enlightenment to the intruders through set teeth:

"Grease paint and make-up are pretty obvious under my very excellent lighting system!"

With a squeal of rage Rita shot forward, clawing at him like a young tigeress.

"You brute!" she cried. "Let her go! You brute!"

"Or I'll have my eyes scratched out, eh? No, thank you, madam!" this firmly to Rita, whose wrists he had caught in a masterful grip, after releasing the other girl.

But his capture of Rita brought the whole half dozen of her comrades upon him like hornets, getting in some stinging blows too, till Rita's voice rose above the clamour.

"No! No! Not six to one, girls! It isn't fair even if he is a man; though he's not a gentleman. Pay him out some other way. Smash something!"

She was free within the next minute. As Coral led her indignant mob, on destruction bent, towards a trestle table that held a miscellany of glass articles, tins, bottles and strange instruments, the man let out a mighty shout:

"Don't touch! for Heaven's sake don't touch!" and with two or three wild leaps he put himself between the would-be destroyers and the table.

"I apologize!" he called out, and the girls, impressed by something in his voice, drew back rather scaredly from the sudden whiteness of his face. "I apologize for losing my temper," he went on after a moment. "If I'm not a gentleman," this with a withering glance for Rita, "at least I've the grace to do that. I should like to remind you at the same time that you haven't conducted yourselves as ladies. I don't know who you are or why you have come ferreting here, but I've no doubt the police will soon find out when I send for them and give you in charge for trespassing."

Six of the girls pulled rather long faces at that threat, but not so Rita; she realized too keenly the necessity of keeping her end up.

"You can telephone them, of course!" she scoffed.

"You think I'm bluffing, I see," he retorted cuttingly. "But, although I have not the convenience of a telephone, I use wireless, and, as for reasons of my own, I happen to be closely in touch with the police, my summons will be speedily answered."

There was a tense silence at that; his confident tone and words carried conviction only too well, and now that he had calmed down the girls were aware of a steady power about him that was very disconcerting to them. With his strong, open face and straight glance, he did not look in the least like a wrong-doer; even Rita had to acknowledge to herself that smuggling or dabbling with black magic were the very last things of which he appeared capable. His broad, high forehead under crisp hair spoke of cleverness. But there was no criminal cunning in his widely spaced eyes, they were dark and deep-looking like shining pools holding secrets in their depths. His suit was of the free-and-easy flannel type, but well made and clean looking, possibly protected through whatever work it was that he did, by one of the long linen coats that lay about.

But in the uncomfortable pause, Rita's quick brain decided that it would never do to let him see he had inspired fright.

Besides, she had drawn the other girls into this impasse with her, and it behoved her to get them out of it. She must try to keep the man in play while they edged out, then she herself would make a wild bolt after them as soon as possible.

So her glance at them was full of meaning, indicating the doorway; then, in spite of the man's non-criminal looks, she turned on him with well-feigned suspicion.

"In touch with the police for reasons of your own! Huh! a likely story, that! I'll wager it's the other way round, that the police have their reasons for keeping you under supervision."

With attention, temporarily, only for the girl who taunted him, the young man moved closer to her, looking ferocious.

"What do you mean?" he demanded, truculently.

Triumphantly aware that her friends were

helping themselves and her by making ready to bolt, she stood her ground and drawled with perfect coolness:

"Exactly what I say, O Man of Mystery. I don't profess to a lot of knowledge in such matters, but I believe I am right in saying that the police kept a wary eye on anyone who has once been—er—through their hands, as one might say."

"Through their hands!" The young man, red in the face now with fury, was shouting in his wrath, quite oblivious of the fact that Coral and Hilary were doing lightning work behind him, shoving up various impediments to trip him up should he suddenly try to head off Rita's impending dash for liberty.

That delighted creature allowed herself a sardonic smile, seemingly at the man, but really at what was going on behind his back.

The smile added fuel to his rage.

"Through their hands!" he bawled again, adding: "What do you take me for? A ticket-of-leave man? A lunatic?"

Rita shrugged delicately, and raised deprecating eyebrows at him.

"I haven't said so," she returned, still cool of eye and with her aggravating drawl. "There may be a dozen reasons for the police and yourself being—er—in touch," she lingered on the last word, giving it a queer significance, before adding quietly, "I don't know!" then let her glance wander all about the laden table he had so jealously sprung forward to guard. "Anyhow," she went on again after the briefest of pauses, and softly as though talking to herself, "newspaper people can make up exciting stories about almost anything."

The man stood glaring at her, hands thrust deeply into his jacket pockets, as if to keep them strictly under control.

"He has got a job not to box my ears," was Rita's perfectly correct reading of his look and attitude, and, not without a tinge of admiration, she noted his determined struggle for mastery over his temper.

"It's apt to give people the whip hand," her thoughts rambled on as she awaited his next move, "when they can rein themselves in and hold tight."

His fight with himself was won, and before

many seconds had passed, too. She saw him relax, but his calm looked more to be reckoned with than his red hot fury had done.

"Before you move out of this cave, young lady," he said, very coldly, "you will apologize humbly to me for your intrusion and your insulting remarks. Take your time! I'm used to standing."

A duel of words and wits! Rita revelled in it, and although aware that direct action could not long be delayed, indulged in a few more words first. Ignoring the last ironic sentences, she said:

"I never apologize unless I'm really in the wrong and not always then. It's just as the fit takes me."

He said nothing to that, and into the silence she added:

"And it doesn't take me—on this occasion."

His look at her was steady and exceedingly grim.

"But no doubt one will, presently," he retorted, and reiterated: "Take your time! I'm used to standing."

Of the other girls, all but Coral and Hilary were now standing close to the cave opening.

Rita's fleeting glance told her that even the latter pair held themselves for flight; Coral significantly held up her wrist watch, too, reminding Rita that it was time to be off or they would be late back at school.

But she could not forbear just one more tilt at the island's mystery man.

"And what about the police? But perhaps you'll prefer to take the law in your own hands, after all. Less embarrassing, eh?"

The young fellow looked daggers at her. "I'll summon the police in my own time," he snapped, "but you can be assured, Miss Pert, that I shall wireless them to take my trespassers."

Rita's glance flickered beyond him then, a warning to her friends as she flung her challenge.

"Wireless for all you're worth, Mr. Mysterious. The police, if they come, will find no trespassers here. Girls! the boat! *Run!*"

CHAPTER IX

THE ISLAND SECRET

BUT, even as everybody poised for flight, the island man's voice rang out arrestingly.

"And the trespassers will find no boat. There will be only the police boat, for their return voyage."

Alarmed eyes met his, and Coral gasped out: "You mean, you've sent her adrift?"

He shook his head. "I've too much respect for another man's property to do that," he replied crushingly.

"Then, you've hidden her?" This from Rita, who got the full benefit of his provoking grin of triumph.

"Yes! and I defy any of you to find her in a month of Sundays. So now, we're as we were, eh, what?"

It was Hilary, out of the badly rattled group, who exploded this time.

"My friend was right," she cried; "you're

not a gentleman; you're nothing but a cad, keeping a picnic party of girls——"

"Oh! oh! oh! a picnic party!" the young man's eyebrows went up. "A picnic party!" he repeated; then he laughed contemptuously. "What's the use of trying a lie like that on me, after what I overheard? You came to spy. To find out what I was up to. Well, what did you suppose I was up to? And what has my business to do with you? You'd better think out answers to those questions all ready for the police."

Rather desperately now Rita again took up her rôle of chief spokeswoman for her party.

"Very well!" she said, levelly and with an assurance she was really far from feeling at the moment. "And you'd better be thinking out reasons to give to the public as to why this island shouldn't be safe at times; why, if people should see red, they mustn't land. Send for the police just as soon as you like, Mr. Mysterious; the sooner the better, so that we girls can all get back and talk, talk, talk, about you and your extremely rummy island. Even the police will find it pretty difficult to prevent hordes of curious people poking here at *all* hours of *all* day and *every* day."

Deadlock! The girls could see in a minute that the man found the position just that. Frowningly silent, he was evidently nonplussed. So Rita, with the desperate need of getting back to school uppermost in her thoughts, followed up her momentary advantage. Sidling nearer to him, she said appealingly: "I say! can't we drop all this, whatever we think of each other? Can't you be a sport and let us go? It can't be so many years ago since you were a schoolboy and got into scrapes. Well, we're schoolgirls and it's going to be pretty awful for us if we're late back, or if we're heard of as in the hands of the police. Be a sport!"

Was there just the faintest twinkle in the eyes that studied the seven sinners? The girls thought so, but kept their faces suitably long and pleading in case they were mistaken.

"Schoolgirls, eh?" he responded cynically. "Shouldn't have thought it. You look more like a crowd of cheap comedy actresses." Then his tone changed, becoming more kindly. "I wouldn't masquerade like that again, if I were you. Schoolgirls! h'm! not from—— Ah-h-h! How did you get hold of something I wrote? That about danger on the island and seeing red? Remarks that were in a private letter to my sister?"

"Your sister!" the words came in a shrieked chorus.

"Yes! Miss Howard! She's a mistress at a school called Camberside, and I bet that's where——"

A universal groan from the girls stopped him, and Rita confessed: "Yes! we're from Camberside right enough. So now we are done; ab-so-lute-ly."

Mr. Howard understood in a second the dire significance in her tone. He smiled. "Not necessarily," was his reassurance. "The price of my silence could be—yours!"

"But supposing our silence would be wrong?" argued Rita, not wishing to climb down too quickly; "supposing you are doing something criminal here? You might be deceiving the police, even if what you said about being in touch with them is true."

"See here!" the young man said vigorously.

"I can tell that the best way of keeping my business here quiet, is to trust you girls *with* it. If I give you all my word of honour not to mention your invasion to my sister, and you give me yours to keep what I tell you entirely to yourselves, what will that amount to?"

"Pax!" announced Rita promptly, and shot out her right hand.

"Right-ho! pax it is!" Mr. Howard endorsed, taking it and then following suit all round.

"The only snag now is that we're frightfully short of time, Mr. Howard," Rita told him. "Can you tell us all about your secret in ten minutes? We ought to be gone from here by then, or we shall be late back at school. We've to catch a bus and transform ourselves, you see."

The young man's smile flashed out again. "I can tell you a lot in ten minutes," he said, and got briskly on with the job.

"I know girls can keep secrets, because I've two splendid sisters whom I can always trust to do so. The elder you know, the younger lives at home with my widowed mother, who is rather an invalid. They're both fine, these sisters of mine, but I must particularly mention

185

what the one *you* know is doing. To give me my chance, she is earning every penny she can, helping to keep the home going and financing me a good deal, too; teaching at Camberside all the week, and actually taking a deputy organist's job at a cinema, though she *hates* that last. She's working too hard, really. You see, she has to keep me going here, too. I don't want attention attracted to the island, so I just get a note of my wants delivered to her by a fisher boy who is only too glad to keep his mouth shut for the tip he gets. Then, so long as she doesn't see my little red flag flying at a point she knows, she comes with my stuff every week-end. The flag means that I'm engaged on dangerous experiments. But I don't like the look of her now, although I had to insist on her having a change at Easter. She's overtaxed, tired out, I'm afraid. She's game, though. I've got to go on; I can't fail her after all her struggles to give me my chance——"

"Well? And what *is* your chance, Mr. Howard?"

Rita broke into a pause during which the narrator had seemed lost in his own thoughts.

186

Abstraction left his face, it became animated again, the face of a doer rather than a dreamer.

"My chance?" he echoed, and went on rapidly:

"Inventing, making a fortune. But trot around with me, all of you. I'll show you my gadgets and explain."

It appeared that young Howard was engaged in an endeavour to make a fortune by the invention of a new explosive which he intended to offer to the British Government. For secrecy's sake and because of the dangerous nature of his work, the money of the Howards had been sunk in the purchase of the little island, where he might experiment without fear of interruption, espionage or risk of damage to others than himself, should those experiments lead to disaster.

All this he told his thrilled listeners as he marched them about his cave domain and laboratory. Evidences of his inventive brain were everywhere, but the girls were especially interested in the contents of the cavern where his chief experiments were carried on, and where he hoped soon to realize his great ambition.

"It's been awfully kind of you to show us round and tell us things as you have done, Mr. Howard," Rita said warmly as he finished his rapid outlining. "I expect we seven all feel as mean as dirt, tracking Miss Howard down as we did to-day. I know *I* do. Horrors! we've been suspecting you of all sorts of things. You won't ever tell her, Mr. Howard, will you? Honour bright."

"Honour bright!" he vowed. "And in return I'm relying on all of you to keep my secret. The police know that I'm an inventor and it's arranged that I wireless them if ever I'm in any sort of trouble; that is," here he grinned cheerfully, "supposing there's enough of me left to *do* the wirelessing. But they don't know anything definite about my ambition, and I wouldn't for worlds have the Press nosing round here. A hint in the newspapers and I might be the unwelcome recipient of attention from abroad."

There were comprehending looks from the girls, to which Coral gave voice.

"Very probably, I should say. Plenty of foreign powers would pay well for what you hope to perfect, Mr. Howard, which means that

188

there might be attempts to steal your secret. Well, it won't be our fault if anything leaks out. We'll be absolutely mum, and do our bit towards helping on the good work by giving your sister at school as little trouble as possible from now on. Won't we, Rita?"

The girl who had instigated the vendetta against Miss Howard, nodded vehemently. "We'll be sports!" she said with a hearty conciseness which told her friends that the vendetta was at an end.

In blithe ignorance of the fact that there had ever been such a bitter animus against his sister, Mr. Howard fairly beamed on his young visitors.

"Now that we're on such good terms," he said genially, "I'm sure you won't think that I want to hurry you off when I remind you of your limited time; it's for your own sakes."

Coral looked at her wrist watch and exclaimed agitatedly:

"Heavens! I say, girls! we've badly outs ayed that ten minutes; we must hustle like mad; our boat, Mr. Howard! Oh, I hope it isn't far off."

He beckoned them after him. "It's nearer and more get-at-able than where you left it," he cried cheerily, "and I don't mind you knowing now about my secret waterway. Come along!"

Much intrigued in spite of their hurry, the girls followed him outside and down a gradual slope about fifty yards, that seemed to lead right into the sea. But, still beckoning reassuringly, he swung himself round a crag several feet above the water.

"Quite safe if you hold on tightly; there's foothold all round," he cried, and a minute later each girl had swung herself after him into a long, low water cavern, inside which they could just discern a small motor boat with their own craft beside it, moored to an iron spike which had been driven immovably into a deep cleft.

"I found this hidey-hole quite by chance when swimming one morning," the young man explained. "And it did me a good turn. I shouldn't have been round this side of the island at all, as a matter of fact, but I got into a strong current and was simply swept round here, rather to my dismay. However, that same current eddied me near this little place and I managed to reach this shelf at the side and clamber back the way we've come. But you can see how safely I could defy you to find your boat. The place isn't noticeable even from the water, unless one is quite close to it, closer than any boat is ever likely to be unless driven in by rough weather."

"It's all marvellous, quite like a story," Rita told him as he held the boat steady for embarkation. "I only wish there was going to be another chapter in it, for us."

The young man laughed. "Perhaps there *will* be; who knows? Anyhow, I shall expect a round robin of congratulation from you all, if you read in the newspapers presently that I've been successful."

"I hope we *shall*. We shall feel proud of having nearly come to fisticuffs with such a celebrity," Coral said. "And you shall have the round robin all right," she added.

"That is, if we haven't all been sacked from Camberside over this little trip," put in Hilary on a cautionary note.

"I say!" Mr. Howard's voice held concern. "*That* mustn't happen, you know. Here!" fishing out a notecase from a pocket, "you take this and hire a taxi if you lose the bus.

You can send me the cash back at any old time. Just shove it in an envelope and address it to me care of Burlton Post Office. I shall get it all right," and simultaneously with his vigorous thrust to the boat, sending it out of the water tunnel, he tossed in a pound note.

It was Rita who picked it up, holding it a loft while her gaze travelled between her friends and the man standing smilingly watching them all.

"We can't take it, can we, girls?" she cried, then as headshakes answered her, she told the donor.

"It's awfully good of you, Mr. Howard, but we really must take our chance of the bus. We wouldn't be able to pay you back at once and we should only worry for fear you were needing it."

But he waved the girls on their way. "Nice of you, knowing that I'm not exactly a millionaire," he called genially, "but I can manage all right, so don't fidget. Remember that it's to my advantage as well as yours, that you all get back to time; no awkward inquiries and what not; a case of one for you and two for myself, don't you see?"

"So *you* say, Mr. Howard, but I know you're really thinking most of us," was Coral's warmly spoken tribute. "Please forgive me for saying a while back that you weren't a gentleman; you're the best ever."

"And so say all of us!" seconded Rita, as she stowed the note safely away in response to his wish before taking to her oar. "Mr. Howard, I *do* apologize, honestly. I'm as sorry as anything for having been so rude to you."

He waved again in great good humour, his voice carrying strongly over the stretch of smacking waves now between him and the boatload of girls.

"That's all right! I wasn't too polite myself, so *I* apologize too. Now we're quits and all jolly good friends, eh what?" and back to his ears floated a full-throated cheer.

Out of sight of the island hermit, rowing ceased for a minute or so to enable the girls to get their bearings, and ere oars were plied again, glances lingered ponderingly on the ocean stronghold that sheltered so stirring a secret.

"My goodness! what a discovery!" murmured Rita. "We shouldn't be feeling much more staggered if we had come across pirates or smugglers, I suppose. We shall jolly well have to guard our tongues with such a secret as this in our possession."

"'Staggered' is the very word," agreed Coral, eloquently "Let's hope that nobody among us talks in her sleep!"

CHAPTER X

REJECTED OVERTURES

THE row back was too strenuous a business to admit of talking, even if the girls had not felt in too much of a whirl for coherent chatter. Just one short discussion took place as the boat drew clear of the island and was headed for the mainland, and then silence reigned during the trip.

"Girls!" Rita said seriously, "we've got to get that bus if it's humanly possible. We know Mr. Howard hasn't any money to spare for loaning and we might not be able to make up anything we borrowed for quite a while after to-day's jaunt. Besides, I've got an idea which will take toll of our pocket money for a bit, so we can't afford to mortgage any of it."

"Some of our next pocket money is mortgaged already; we're all in your debt; in spite of what you said the other day, we don't feel we can let you stand the racket of all this," Coral said.

"Oh, yes, you can," argued Rita. "I've had more than my money's worth of excitement to-day. We'll just call the financial side of this trip square and look forward to our next. Now! *Pull!*"

Almost superhuman effort went to the catching of that bus, but the girls felt no inclination to whine over strained muscles and blistered hands when, with barely a minute to spare, they clambered breathlessly aboard it. Even the fact that there had been no time for the badly-needed refreshments could not depress them. For something had happened to break the monotony of term time. They had a secret in common which would have the power to keep them in a state of constant speculation. They thought they had stumbled on the reason for Miss Howard's 'jumpiness,' and discussed it at some length that night in the seclusion of Rita's cubicle.

"Without knowing it," Coral said sagely, "Miss Howard will be like a weathercock to us, showing which way the wind is blowing as regards the island affair. There's no doubt that all her tantrums lately are due to the strain of it; she's all keyed up, I expect, wondering what will happen next, and has to vent her nerviness on somebody or burst."

"And of course, *we* haven't made things any easier for her lately; we've all been playing her up in one way or another."

"All through me," Rita cut in upon Hilary's rather rueful utterance. "No! don't look apologetic, Hil. I quite understand that you didn't mean it that way. But it's true; you know very well that I worked you all up against her, and I wish I hadn't, now that I know what she's really like. Whether I care for people or not, I always admire the ones who *do* things, and in spite of my grievance against her I've got to admit to myself that she's fine, helping her brother and keeping her home going as she's doing. Don't imagine that I've become angelic all at once because I'm talking like this; she may say or do something to-morrow that will make me mad again, but, all the same, I'm going to try and be decent to her in future."

"And you expect us to do likewise, I suppose?" the query came a trifle satirically from Olive Gray, one of the "chosen."

Rita sent a long, measuring look the round of her friends.

"I don't expect *anything*," she replied quietly. "It's up to you all to do as you choose. But as I was the girl to start the feud against Miss Howard, it's only right that I should tell you the line *I* mean to take from now on."

"And it's one that *I'm* going to take too, Rita," Coral said, very decidedly. "I liked you enough to follow your lead in the crazy campaign, and as I like you even more now, I'll back you up in a reform."

"Reform!" echoed Olive with disgust, and several mouths turned down dejectedly.

Rita laughed, then nodded her burnished head at the malcontents. "Don't worry!" she bade them dryly. "It won't be as bad as it sounds. The Rita reform applies only to treatment of Miss Howard, so you needn't run away with the idea that it means cutting out any more jaunts."

The significance of this statement fully restored any wavering allegiance on the part of the "chosen." They were one broad grin, and Olive observed complacently: "Good! we won't mind making ourselves amiable to Miss Howard in the circumstances, but we *do* bar going back to positive stagnation. Your coming to Camberside may not be an unmixed blessing from the point of view of the mistresses, Rita, but it has jolly well livened things up for us."

"Well!" Rita drawled, pleased in spite of her careless manner. "I'm not a chameleon, so there won't be much change in me, I can promise you. I shall simply *have* to ginger things up while I'm here. Don't forget that I've already dropped a hint of a new project."

Her hearers looked blank inquiry for a moment or two, but at her impatient: "Yes! in the boat; don't you remember?" their cautiously modulated exclamations burst out.

"So you did!"

"Of course!"

"What is in the wind?"

Willingly enough, she proceeded to enlighten them.

"We shall have to wait a week or two, till we are in funds again, and, of course, it's subject to you all agreeing. I thought it would be an awfully nice idea to treat Mr. Howard, say, to some chocolate, baccy and cigars. I expect he loves to smoke over his problems; when he isn't actually experimenting, I mean. Daddy always says he gets inspiration out of his pipe. But about Mr. Howard; it struck me that a little offering of the kind I've mentioned would make up to him for our spying on him and his sister, nosing into their affairs as we did, and show him how we appreciated his not giving us away to her. Heaven knows what sort of a row Juppy would have made if he had reported us to her. I'm certain it would have ended in my being docked of Tommy, and I'm duly grateful to Mr. Howard for keeping our secret."

"And so say all of us, *I'm* sure!" Coral received the prompt confirmatory nods she expected as she glanced inquiringly at the other five adventuresses. "As for *his* secret, the tortures of the Inquisition wouldn't get it out of me. Rita, we're with you to a girl over the 'treating.' But how shall we get the stuff? It would be too risky to try shopping at Mother Dodge's for tobacco and cigars; you know what a strict old soul she is; she might be putting out feelers to the mistresses about such purchases."

"My goodness!" exclaimed Rita in lively horror. "I hadn't even *dreamed* of Mother Dodge in this connection. For one thing, I don't suppose she's got a cigar in the place. And anyhow, it would never do to shop *there* except for the chocolate; we could give her that custom safely enough. No! my idea is for another town trip, with a boat to the island."

Startled sounds from her friends gave her pause here, but she went on almost immediately and with the utmost calmness:

"I don't see that there's anything to gasp about. The same clothes will do again; it's absurd to have gone to risk and trouble over them for just one jaunt, and if we pool the bus and boat expenses, it won't amount to much each."

"N-no! and we'd love to go, of course," this with dawning excitement from Hilary. "The drawback is, I'm afraid there isn't enough grease paint and make-up for another 'do' for all of us. We rather laid it on to-day, you know."

"I *do*, to my cost!" Rita smoothed her cheeks discontentedly. "It's been a frightful job getting it right off and I hate the beastly stuff on me at all."

"I daresay, with *your* complexion"; Hilary looked with admiring envy at Rita's lovely colouring. "But perhaps it's as well that some people's are hidden a bit."

Rita laughed. "I'll return your compliment by saying that none of you others need worry; we've all got decent faces, as faces go, so, as Mr. Howard knows we're from Camberside, there's no reason why he shouldn't see them as they are next time. Let's just tie coloured scarves round our heads as additional disguise for bus and town, and chance our faces. Mr. Howard evidently thought we looked a pretty cheap lot, and, speaking for myself, I'd like to give him a little better impression. I don't know what you think."

But she knew an instant later. There wasn't a girl among the other six who was not anxious to cut a better figure in the eyes and estimation of the young inventor into whose hermitage they had trespassed.

"Right! then that's settled," cried Rita in a satisfied tone. "And next week we'll start our peace campaign on behalf of Miss Howard."

But a rude awakening was in store for the girl

whose malignance towards the English mistress had had such a demoralizing effect upon the school. Rita was to find, as many others in the world have found, that the flame of revolution, once lit, is very hard to quench. In the case of Camberside, quite a number of girls had sufficient of the riotous element in them to be thoroughly stirred up by one of Rita's calibre; apart from her personal attraction, they welcomed her as a breaker of monotony, somebody who added a spice of the unexpected to the dullness of their ordered existence; she "leavened the lump" as one girl had been heard to remark. And on the wave of tempestuousness, many of her quieter schoolfellows had been carried along, getting a deal of pleasure out of being "in the swim," even in the perilous waters of rebellion.

So, astonishment at Rita's sudden change of front, absolutely unaccountable except to her faithful six, was soon followed by a good deal of cynical speculation as to the cause of it. Ideas were bandied about freely, often within earshot of the would-be reformers, and even when tongues were guarded, sidelong glances conveyed suspicion and curiosity. As Rita's altered demeanour in class time became more apparent, remarks were passed that astounded the half dozen girls who were following her new lead. Coral, who had once predicted that Rita's leadership would prevail in *any* circumstances, had to admit herself mistaken.

"I would have sworn that Rita could have swayed opinion any way she chose," she told Hilary.

But the latter pursed her lips and shook her head as she replied: "She would in the ordinary way, I feel sure, but I think she's been too much of a quick-change artist in this act. The girls are bewildered, rather naturally. You see, she can't give them a really plausible reason for wanting to treat Miss Howard nicely all at once; they think she's being made to sing small by somebody, and they don't see why they should do the same at her bidding. If they knew what we do! But there's the rub, they don't; and they won't, either, because, being under a bond of secrecy, we can't enlighten them."

"H'm! it's a very queer position for everybody," Coral said, thoughtfully. "A lot of the

204

girls think we seven are trying to curry favour
with Miss Howard for some unknown reason.
But I should think that idea would soon be
dispelled if they're not too dense to notice how
she treats us, and Rita especially. I expect *you*
have caught that gimlet gleam in her eyes which
she reserves for us, with a sort of double strength
for Rita?"

Hilary shrugged. "Rather! It has made me
wonder if she can possibly know anything about
our trip. But she can't, can she? Mr. Howard
looked such a straight sort. I couldn't imagine
him breaking faith with us, could *you?*"

"Hardly!" Coral opined. "Although now that
you've broached the subject, I'll admit that I've
felt a trifle uneasy in case he felt it a duty to have
a watch set on us. He *might* have given his sister
warning, on the understanding that she didn't
give us away to Juppy or say a word to us."

Hilary groaned dolefully. "It's a possibility,
worse luck, but for heaven's sake, let's keep it
to ourselves. If Rita had any such misgiving,
goodness knows what she would do, something
frightfully rash in a blazing temper, probably.
In fact, I believe she's beginning to feel huffy

already, because Miss Howard isn't exactly doing a fatted-calf-for-the-returned-prodigal stunt."

It happened that this canny conjecture of Hilary's was not far from the truth. There was a big streak of generosity in Rita that even her imperious temper and strong self-will could not entirely smother. That generosity had come uppermost in response to the story of Miss Howard's endeavours, and was the urge which had driven her to capitulation. If she could do nothing to help, at least she wished to do nothing to hinder. Not only that, but nobody else must hinder either, by making term time difficult for the woman who was working so hard in an important cause. All this was easy enough to think out, but not so easy of accomplishment. Rita was chagrined to notice that her more tractable mood made no difference whatever to Miss Howard's attitude; she was still as distant in manner as she had been of late, still as fault-finding and sharp tempered. But it was not long before Rita blamed the majority of the girls for this; they were adhering to the breakaway to which she herself had incited them, pouring scorn on the weak-kneed figure of speech which she gave as the reason for her altered outlook. The remark: "I've decided that she isn't worth baiting any longer," didn't sound a bit convincing, coming without the slightest warning whatever from "that terror, Rita Conway." The girls were sure that a totally different interpretation could be given to her changeableness, and were incensed because it was withheld from them. So the tension between "Rita's *v.* The Rest!" as Hilary tersely put it, was great, creating an atmosphere of vague disquiet throughout the school.

CHAPTER XI

POSSIBLY the ferment affected Miss Howard; at any rate, it was with a depressed and dissatisfied air that she sat in the big cave on the island, talking to her brother, on the Saturday a fortnight later than the one on which she had been followed there by the searching seven.

As chance had it, she was thinking of Rita and her little coterie when her brother inquired solicitously:

"Anything wrong, Grace? You've looked a bit hipped lately, to my idea. Look here! I've asked you before. What *is* it? I'm afraid you're doing too much."

Too dispirited just then to keep up the usual fiction of "I'm quite all right!" she drew a hand wearily across her eyes.

"It isn't that, Jack. I can stand plenty of work. I'm just nervy and not sleeping well, that's all."

"That's *all!*" he echoed, adding vigorously: "Takes in a good deal, I should say. Lack of sleep plays the deuce with anyone. You're over-done, that's the trouble; I oughtn't to have gone on so long with my experiments, but I'll just shut up shop here and take that worry off your mind."

"No! no! Jack, you mustn't. It isn't that!" Miss Howard's tone was agitated. "It's only that I'm silly, hyper-sensitive, I suppose——"

The young man looked on in bewildered consternation as she suddenly broke off and began to cry.

"Here! I say!" he burst out at length, after allowing her to "get it over" as he mentally termed it, for a minute or two. "It's the doctor and a nerve tonic for you this very day, and I'm coming over with you to see him myself. I can see I'm being selfish messing about here while you're slogging so hard to keep everything going."

Miss Howard gave one final dab at her eyes, then determinedly tucked her handkerchief away and pulled herself together.

"You're not selfish, Jack," she cried, still a little tremulously but with decision all the same. "I'm an idiot! that's what is the matter. Don't

o   209

dare to talk of giving up here, unless, of course, you are tired of trying out things and want to."

"Great heavens, no!" The young man looked aghast at the very idea. "As a matter of fact, old girl," here his expression grew eager, "I think I'm really on the right track with a new formula I'm working at. But I simply won't go on with it unless you tell me who or what has been upsetting you. School? the cinema? Is mother worse? Come on! out with it, and then for a tonic, mind."

His sister gave him an affectionate little nod of reassurance.

"This is all the tonic I need, just to blurt out things for a few minutes, 'let off steam' as you would say. I don't expect you to understand my having allowed a schoolgirl to upset me, but anyhow, you can just have patience while I storm a bit; it will do me good," and into Jack Howard's wondering ears was poured the tale of Rita's defection and bad effect upon the school.

"Don't let her play up like that. Get the little wretch turned out," he put in once during the plaint.

But Miss Howard shook her head. "I hate to think of doing that. I told you, if you remember, how kind the Conways were to me on my holiday; they are such delightful people. That's why I tried so hard to get Rita's affection, for their sakes. I tried till I was out of all patience. Now, she seems changing round, she and the six other girls whom she appears to have positively enslaved, are behaving like lambs."

"H'm!" Jack growled, his brows drawn together in a heavy frown, "The jades see they have gone as far as they dare and have pulled up before you report them."

Miss Howard shook her head again. "I can't think so! I wish I could! No! I believe Rita is coaching them up in some new devilry. She knows, they all do, that they've given me nothing definite to report; it has just been an insidious persecution, a kind of mental pin-pricking, which has driven me almost to desperation. I expect that girl's idea is to torture me into leaving Camberside, her revenge for what she imagines was my pressure on her parents. It all seems ridiculous, but to a person with a lot of work and anxiety on her mind, a situation like that can be deadly. Why! one night a little while ago, I couldn't bring myself to go to bed until I had gone to the school chapel and played through some of my organ pieces."

Her brother stared. "Great Scot! Why? I should have thought you had enough of them at the cinema."

"Of course I do! Ugh! hateful job!" Miss Howard's tone was disgusted. "Still, I'm glad of it to help us," she went on. "If you had known the panic I was in that night when I suddenly felt that I shouldn't be able to continue it, that my memory had failed and that I'd forgotten my music notes! Extraordinary, wasn't it? The sleeplessness, of course, from all the worry and irritation I was enduring and keeping all to myself. Well, I waited till after midnight and then off I prowled to the chapel, feeling frightfully nerve-racked, though reassured after I had proved my powers. But supposing I had been seen, Jack! I should have been thought *mad*. So you see what a vindictive schoolgirl *can* do. I wish I could grow a thicker skin," and Miss Howard mustered a little laugh at herself.

Her brother did not join in it. He had been paying close attention to her story and now he inquired thoughtfully: "What's she like, this Rita kid?"

"To look at, do you mean? Oh! charming, quite a picture girl, with a mass of short auburn curls and the loveliest complexion. It's such a pity that her disposition doesn't match her looks; the very attractiveness of those were bound to prove a draw to the other girls, but, unfortunately, with the regrettable results I have mentioned."

"H'm-m-m! a pity, as you say," came reflectively from the young man; his mind's eye was busy calling up a description of the seven young spies with whom he had recently made a pact. Seven of them! Undoubtedly all out that day to flummox his sister! And one of them stood out as plainly in his memory as if she were still facing him, in front of her companions in defiance, with big, fearless eyes that no disguise could alter, looking out of a bedaubed face. He found himself nodding confirmation of his own guesswork, then came out of abstraction to glance sharply at his sister and was relieved to note that her gaze was not upon him at that moment.

"What sort of eyes?" he queried, with seeming carelessness; he had recalled the fact that the hair of the spy leader had been enmeshed in a thick net arrangement, but he distinctly remembered noticing a reddish gleam through it, and also an escaping tendril that was curly. Still, he wanted to be *quite* sure of his ground.

His sister looked surprised. "Whose? Rita's, do you mean? Oh! golden-brown, rather wonderful, really, but looking as if they would challenge the world. Why do you ask."

The young man waved his hand airily. "Just idle curiosity. They sound quite good from a character study point of view. I'd trust them if I were you."

"For what?" Miss Howard asked a trifle sharply.

"To say she's playing the game by you now," her brother urged quietly. "She probably is, you know. And I advise you not to put her off it by appearing suspicious of her seeming good intentions. Give her a chance! Give the whole lot of them a chance."

She sat looking at him for a full minute, weighing his words.

"I oughtn't to be so suspicious," she said at last. "I *ought* to be more charitable, and yet, I can't believe in such a quick reform in those girls; it's been absolutely sudden, you know, Jack. It puzzles me."

"Then don't let it puzzle you any longer," he replied. "No doubt the girl Rita and her crowd feel that they've had their fling; they've been letting off steam in their way probably, just as you have been doing in yours; and now they're feeling better;" he smiled cheerily at her as he added, "I hope *you* are going to feel better, too, now."

Miss Howard returned his smile. "It won't be your fault if I don't, Jack," she said. "I'm rather ashamed to have bothered you with such a tale of woe; schoolgirl peccadilloes must seem trivial to you. But you have cheered and encouraged me. I've been so afraid of breaking down and having to give up Camberside, which would be a tragic business as things are at the moment. Now I must really be off back, or mother will think you've blown us both up."

The young man walked beside her with a comradely hand on her shoulder. "Just keep

those words in mind, old girl, and carry on. I'm
near my goal; I'm certain of it. Once reached,
nothing shall be spared to get mother back to
health and you free of any more cinema stunts
and Cambersiding."

"Oh, no! not the last, Jack, I hope," Miss
Howard demurred. "I love my work, and I've
been very happy at Camberside until these last
few weeks. If you make the fortune you hope to,
so that you and Evelyn can be married and take
mother abroad for a while as you have planned,
I want to stay on at Camberside, if the girls
don't make it unbearable for me. Anyhow, I'll
keep your advice in mind and try to believe in
the great transformation," and she finished up
with a brightened face.

Jack Howard, alone again presently on his
rocky hermitage, muttered to himself: "I hope
I've put everybody on the right road to peace.
But, by gad! if I had those prying wretches here
just now, I'd wring their necks with the greatest
pleasure in life, for giving Grace such a time
of it."

All the same, a wide grin accompanied the
dire words as he returned to his risky job.

CHAPTER XII

DRAMATIC HAPPENINGS

MR. CONWAY, senior, was puzzling his way through a letter written in the most appalling scrawl. But he didn't seem to be minding the tax on his vision and his guessing powers, for his eyes held their usual whimsicality and his lips twitched amusedly. After the mental struggle, he deciphered as follows:

"*Dearest Grandpa,*

"*I hope you and Auntie Sara are well. I am, as usual. But to get to the point. School is a frightfully expensive place. I shall need a small fortune to keep me going respectably in it. In spite of the pocket money I started with, not much, it's true, and a bit I had to ask Mummy and Daddy for later, I haven't a bean. And it's awful to be absolutely stoney when one has real demands on one, sort of debts of honour and so on. What I need cash for at the moment is for what I might call a thank offering for mercies received. Anyway, it is to buy a thank offering and the mercies I may be able to tell you about later. At present, it's all a secret, but I'm sure you would thoroughly approve if you knew, and consider me honoured to be trusted with such a secret. You might almost look on it in this way, too, that I can't be a bad sort for anyone to have done such a thing. So, Grandpa, I am wondering if you will oblige me with a loan off what you always give me at Christmas? I won't a bit mind going short then. Or, if you don't like the idea of waiting so long for a square up, perhaps you will lend me a few shillings (ten or so would do at a pinch) just till I get home at the end of the term; I'll sell some of my rabbits then and pay you back. Only I* don't *feel I ought to write home for any more money just yet; Mummy and Daddy will think I'm sowing wild oats or something. Jimmy says that* always *runs away with heaps of money, he's heard chaps say. I hate to bother you, Grandpa dear, but if I am ever able to tell you all the ins and outs of this secret I'm in, you will be glad that you helped so tremendously with a mere loan.*

"Your loving grand-daughter,
"Rita."

After laboriously picking out every word, Mr. Conway, senior, threw back his head and indulged in a guffaw of laughter that quickly brought his niece's head round the door of the sunny little room in which they breakfasted together.

"What's the great joke, Uncle?" was her smiling inquiry.

He patted Rita's effusion. "A letter from the fire-eater at Camberside; you shall read it presently, my dear, if you *can*, but you needn't touch on the loan question in it before the folks at the farm. That's between Rita and me. I'm a quarter of an hour early, I see; time to pop down to the post office for a postal order," and the old man stumped off, still chuckling.

Over breakfast he and his niece discussed Rita's appeal.

"Then you're going to grant it, Uncle?" she queried rather dubiously.

But there was no doubt in the old man's face or voice. "Yes!" he said. "After all, curiosity doesn't die with youth and it's my only hope of ever hearing about the great idea."

So, next day, Rita was the recipient of a letter from her grandfather, enclosing a twenty shilling postal order. The letter ran in this wise:

"*My dear Rita,*

"*I am sending you this money as an 'extra,' for three reasons. One is that I don't like loans; never borrow, my dear, if you can possibly avoid doing so; besides, if you sold your rabbits, I should only have to buy them back from whomever you sold them to, to give you peace of mind regarding their having a good home. Another reason is that I should like to feel I had paid my way into the wonderful secret if you are at liberty to share it with me later. And my third reason is the most serious and import-ant one. I trust your word that you are going to pay with*

the money, or part of it, shall we say?—something which
you feel ought to be paid. So count the enclosed gift from
me to be in a good cause. I am sure I shall be very inter-
ested by anything that you can divulge when you come
home, but don't dare to tell me that, with the squandering
of money like water, secrets and mercies, you are not
enjoying school life! Why! you have even forgotten to
mention Tommy in your letter!

> *"Love from*
> *"Grandpa Conway."*

It was Rita's turn to smile over a letter;
but the smile soon faded, leaving her face unusually earnest looking.

"Grandpa *is* a dear!" was her warm thought.
"I'd like to be able to tell him all about everything. I shall ask Mr. Howard if I may, in strict
confidence. Grandpa would be only one extra
in the secret and he would keep it all right.
How glorious, though if it hadn't to be a secret
at all by the time I go home!"

To her friends she bore the news that she had
had a windfall.

"Though, as a matter of fact, it's one I
angled for," she confessed. "But with one or
two birthdays cropping up in the Form to be
celebrated as they have done, our plans for
reparation seemed doomed. So I was desperate.

Now we can make our amends to Mr. Howard next Saturday, and a jolly substantial one it can be."

Another dodging of games put Rita and company on their townward way once more as planned, looking the same in some respects, but vastly different in the one of facial decoration, as on their previous venture.

The seven were in perfect accord that, in view of the "windfall," no meagre thank offering should be presented to their hero of the island. Only the strictly necessary expenses entailed by travel thereto and the simplest tea fare calculated to appease well-controlled appetites, were to be allowed; the balance of the pound was to be offered up as compensation for spying and thanks for counsel kept.

But this decision brought need for caution in its train.

"We can't possibly surge into a tobacconist's shop and buy up a whole lot of stuff," was Coral's objection. "We should attract just the attention we are anxious to avoid not having disguised faces this time. We look like school-girls now, in spite of our grown-up frocks, and

Rita's hair might give us away anywhere, to anyone. It's extraordinary how things get to the ears of the mistresses, and one of them lives in Burlton, don't forget."

"We aren't likely to," Rita growled. "I'm absolutely face conscious, all because of that thought, at every corner we come to. I feel myself all eyes, expecting to collide with Miss Howard by some contrary fate. But you're quite right about the shopping, Carol, and I vote we divide the money up between us and each buy at a different shop, having first settled *what* to ask for. After all, we shall be distributing our custom, doing all the tobacconists a good turn."

It took some little time, this tracking down of seven different shops, but it was managed at last, and after buns and tea "to restore the wasted tissues," to quote Rita, the seven made their eager way towards the river, having decided on the patronage of a different boatman, too, from the last occasion.

Their road took them past the very bungalow from near which they had seen Miss Howard put off to the island, and luck favoured them

222

with a wind from the water, as they slowly passed the tamarisk hedge through which they got stray glimpses of a lady lying on a wicker couch in the bungalow garden.

"Grace!" they heard her call.

Then the wind wafted to their ears in Miss Howard's well-known voice: "Coming, Mother dear. What is it?"

"Isn't it time for you to go to Jack?"

Breathlessly the dawdling girls listened for the answer.

"No! I'm to wait for a parcel to arrive at the station, at his special request. He is expecting it on the six o'clock train, so I told him I would fetch it and be at the island about seven. I'm free for some time yet, you see, so we'll have tea out here as the day is so warm for you."

The girls passed on rapidly after that, and at a safe distance from the Howard domain, Rita exclaimed:

"Hallelujah! that disposes of the one snag in our outing. I was so afraid sheer cussedness would land us on the island just when *she* happened to be there. Blessings on Mr.

Howard's parcel; now for a carefree trip to take him *ours!*"

Carefree! The word was to recur to her memory presently under conditions that were far removed from that happy state.

But the boating party, with no misgivings to mar their little voyage, sang light-heartedly as they put distance between themselves and the island. They had just begun the Canadian Boat song. "Row, brothers, row, the stream runs fast!" rang out their fresh young voices, only to break off into startled shrieks as a dull booming sound reached their ears from the island, and as their heads were turned to look towards it, they saw a hurtle of broken rock high in the air. It fell, and all was silence, except for the lap of the waves around their boat.

Glances met hurriedly, each girl saw that the faces of her companions had gone strangely white; each girl shivered apprehensively.

"Put it into action! Row! row! That was an explosion!" Rita burst out pantingly, and over the waves, headed now straight for the little harbour, the boat was propelled by a

224

desperate strength that nearly lifted her clear of the water.

"What shall we find? Oh! what *shall* we find?" Hilary cried agitatedly as they beached the boat.

"For heaven's sake, don't get hysterical," snapped Rita, "or you won't be a bit of good if there has been an accident. There may *not* have been, of course. We shall probably find Mr. Howard smoking calmly after trying out one of his formulas."

They were brave words and her companions knew it; understood that the rasp in the first sentence was due to the same fear that Hilary had voiced, that the leisurely drawl of the latter ones was meant to cover up that fear, and give herself and the rest of them time to rally all their self-control.

"Are we ready?" she inquired after a minute, but the others noticed that her own "readiness" left her empty handed, the thank offering was to be left in the boat, for the time being. Hearts beat with a wildness not to be accounted for by the climb, which was one of easy gradient on this side up to the caves.

But now the caves seemed non-existent. Trembling legs carried quivering bodies hither and thither, glances flashed fearfully here and there and at last eyes met, horror in every pair of them.

"They were about here, the caves! Can he have been—buried?"

Rita had to moisten dry lips with her tongue before she could employ it to say: "Don't! it's too awful to *think!* Hunt on!"

She herself brought the frantic search to an end presently with a horror-stricken cry and a pointing finger that directed downwards, to where, on a rocky ledge far below, lay a motionless body.

In quite a petrified way, the seven aghast girls stood looking down at it, watching in an awful fascination the break of the waves against the ledge of rock, the crawling, spumy fingers of the water reaching up and up its slight slope, till the longest of them touched the still form lying so helplessly there. Soon, perhaps, the ledge would be completely awash, and then—the girls shuddered as they saw in imagination the body slipping farther and farther, drawn down and down by the pitiless waves, until at length it was afloat, being carried away, they could not tell whither.

It was that terrifying realization which galvanized Rita into action.

"I've got to get down there! He may be alive!" she burst out.

Coral shuddered again. "*Can* he be, do you think? He must have been blown up with the rocks and thrown down there. I think he must be—dead."

"But if he isn't?" Rita persisted. "People have such marvellous escapes. Supposing he's only hurt or stunned! We're watching him be carried away, drowned. Oh! I must go down. I *must!* I've got to do it, somehow."

Not one among her chums attempted expostulation. For one thing, they knew it would be useless; Rita would take no notice of them if her mind was made up. For another, they were aware that the hazardous step must be taken; they could not stand there, a gaping crowd, seeing the young inventor, whether dead or alive, either drifting out to sea or perhaps being dashed to and fro, between the jagged rocks.

"But I don't know how you're going to manage it, Rita," Coral said worriedly, her gaze making anxious examination of the dangerous rock slopes which a climber must negotiate. "If only we had a rope for you to hold to," she went on, "we others would feel we were doing something too, if only hanging on to a life-line. I expect we could have found enough things in the caves to knot up, but they seem entirely wrecked."

"So it's no use wasting time thinking about them. I'm off *now!*" As she spoke, Rita let her legs down over the precipitous edge and began feeling for foothold.

But suddenly Hilary shot forward and grabbed her by the shoulder.

"Wait! wait! I saw ropes the other day. There may be one about," she cried urgently.

"But it will take time to see; every minute is precious. I can't wait!" and Rita shook off the staying hand.

Another took its place, however, as Hilary sped away shouting: "I'll look around! *Do* wait!"

Carol tightened her grip on the impatient

Rita. "Yes! *do!*" she counselled. "A rope would make all the difference. If you fell! think of it! Everything would be so much worse, because I think you're the only one of us with the head and nerve for this job."

"Five minutes, then," Rita unwillingly conceded. "It *may* be quicker in the end if there does happen to be a rope," and she drew her legs up again, realizing the unwisdom of keeping that perilous position longer than was necessary.

That was a long pause to the waiting girls whose eyes were drawn, as if by magnetic influence, down to the narrow ledge below. The thrash of the waves sounded ominous to them in their nerve-racked condition, the cry of passing sea gulls seemed like a dirge.

A shout from Hilary startled them all just before the five minutes were gone; she came running as fast as the roughness of the ground and the big tarry coil would let her, and the waiting mob simply fell on the rope in a body.

"Oh, thank Heaven!" breathed Coral.

"Wind your end round something to help bear the strain," Rita enjoined. "I won't dare to bear on it, otherwise, for fear of pulling some of you headlong. Besides, Mr. Howard may be able to climb up by it presently."

A frail hope! But it heartened everybody wonderfully for the task ahead. Even a couple of girls whose dread of heights made it impossible for them to watch Rita's dizzy descent, were able to put into practice their desire to be useful, by holding on to the stiff clumsy knots that tied their rope end round a rugged mound.

"Oh, *pray* it's long enough!"

The agitated murmur came from Coral as she and Hilary, who were nearest the edge, strained forward to watch the hand over hand progress of their plucky schoolfellow. They could not conjecture how far the rope would reach; Rita herself was unable to tell, either. All she could do was to cling to it pantingly as she swung from foothold to foothold, kicking it downward whenever a spur or shelf had checked it into a heap. Anxiously she watched each foot of it as she descended, desperately hoping that no frayed strands would disclose themselves. The farther she descended the more her doubts grew as to whether she could have got far without the rope. There were places where she had to dangle by it, trusting to its next swing inwards for her next hold upon the rocks, and she began to wonder uneasily whether anyone but a monkey would be capable of swarming up, so holed and split was the cliff face.

Her heart gave a jump at last, when, with the ledge her next step down and just enough rope to let her make it, she saw blood beneath her feet. Then Mr. Howard *was* hurt, and badly, she was sure, from the ghastliness of his face, although she had enough knowledge of accidents through farm mishaps not to attach too much importance to the sight of blood. People and animals could bleed quite a lot, she knew, without being in imminent danger of dying.

But no sooner had she reached her precarious position on the narrow platform, than her mouth tightened at the anxiety before her. The blood was pumping from a wound in Mr. Howard's wrist, and she knew that it must be stopped immediately. But how? with nothing to aid her and the necessity of keeping her hold on the rope? Almost choked with the wild beating of her own heart she fumbled to feel his and breathed a great sigh of relief to find that it was beating comparatively strongly. Thankfully she told herself that he was young and robust; provided there were no other more serious injuries, there would be nothing against his getting all right again. But that hæmorrhage must be stopped and aid procured for his rescue.

She jerked out her handkerchief from her sleeve, but returned it with a shake of her head. A bit grubby; she remembered having rubbed her hot palms on it after the rowing. Then her gaze fell on a waving mass that floated on an incoming wave. Seaweed! Ha! iodine was extracted from that, she knew, so it ought to be safer to use than a dirty handkerchief. Grabbing as the wave flung its brown burden along the ledge, she bound some of the seaweed tendrils round the young man's wrist, then pressed her own fingers tightly over them and the wound.

Not until then did she look upwards at her friends.

"I wonder if they'll hear?" she muttered and shouted: "Can't come up! Get help quickly."

Up above the girls were conferring frantically.

"She's shouting something, but I can't catch a word," Coral wailed. "Can anybody else?"

Heads were shaken despairingly, so Coral made a sudden resolve.

"I'll go down too, near enough to hear, anyhow," she cried. "If she could do it, I can. I *will!* I *will!*"

What the resolution meant to her the others could tell by the beads of perspiration showing on her forehead as she started. But lower and lower she ventured, centring her thoughts on the two below needing aid, to keep her mind off the sickening descent.

Added courage came to her with the sound of Rita's words, plain enough to be heard now that only a few feet separated them.

"I can't come up. Holding my fingers over a torn artery to stop bleeding. I know you can drive a car, Coral. Could you manage his motor boat, for help, do you think? It would be quick. You *must* be quick."

"I believe so. Yes, I'm sure I could. I'll *do* it," cried Coral.

"Bravo! Go quickly. Our boat's too slow; besides, the others can't leave the rope. I'm keeping him from being washed off at present, but if the waves get any bigger——" Rita's voice broke off abruptly, then added urgently: "Go! go! Miss Howard and a doctor! Ambulance men; anybody! But be *quick!*"

Hilary told Coral afterwards that she really did come up the rope like a monkey. The miracle to Coral herself was that she hadn't broken her neck, for she had no subsequent recollection of her feet touching anywhere on the way up. On the other girls she spent about five seconds for a few gasped out sentences, then she was off at breakneck speed, murmuring to herself: "If only it's ready! It *must* be ready!"

Those words as she ran, really escaped her in a kind of desperation, for panic had seized upon her immediately the motor boat was mentioned, although she dared not confess that to the heroic girl who was facing such dire peril herself in her endeavours to keep life in the young inventor. Certainly Coral could drive a car; in fact, she had quite a boyish interest in engines, but the very knowledge she had managed to glean about them by various tinkerings upon occasion, warned her now of

234

her limitations. There were engines *and* engines; because she could manage one in a motor car was not to say that she could do the same in a motor boat. Horse-loving Rita scorned and detested "smelly, greasy engines," and had not the remotest idea of their construction or working. Cars, buses and trains were just convenient modes of locomotion and that was all—to her.

But, "You must be quick!" she had said, with such urgency in her voice and anxious eyes that Coral knew it was a matter of life and death. She had implicit faith in Rita's nerve and ability to first-aid, but even those qualities were of small avail when a doctor's skill was sorely needed.

Combined with these worries was distress at the havoc wrought by the explosion. A mental picture of the caves, now a grave of buried hopes, she supposed, came into her mind; mournfully her thoughts dwelt on the blow that must soon fall on the Howard household ashore, the sense of frustration and disappointment to which the inventor must awaken, if he ever did recover. If! the word spurred her on. There must be no "if"; he must be succoured quickly and given the chance of "trying again" in his great ambition.

But her heart sank when, a minute or so later, she looked down at the crag which hid his secret waterway. The force of the explosion had hurled a big boulder against it, not only blocking access to it, but shattering it extensively, as she could see. No doubt the debris could be cleared and a way made again eventually, but that would be a job for several men; she could do nothing about it. How could she reach the motor boat? And if she managed it, supposing she found that damaged, too? There were no footholds by which she could climb over the boulder, the side presented to her being as smooth and rounded as a marble. Desperately, feeling that every second was precious, she looked about for another way of approach to the splintered crag. Could she do the precipitous climb down on the other side of the rough track and swim round the crag into the waterway? Involuntarily, looking at the swirling turbulence of the water thereabouts, she shivered. She might manage the climb at risk to neck or limb, but she knew instinctively that her swimming strength would not be equal to the powerful undertow; she would be swept out and away like a feather.

Inspiration suddenly came to her, however. From the left side of the track she could scale the rocky part beneath which the water bored and made the natural boathouse; she could get beyond the crag that way and drop off the top of the water tunnel. That would necessitate but a few strokes to get her alongside the motor boat; she must just trust to Providence that it was still there and undamaged.

It was a nerve-racking scramble, but an even more trying business was the drop from the overhang of rock into the deep, green water surging restlessly in and out of the tunnel. She dared not stop to look at it or her courage would have failed her; over the rock edge she slid in haste, to strike out immediately she reached the water.

If frightful anxiety had allowed her breath enough, she would have shouted with relief to see the motor boat, seemingly intact, inside its rocky haven, and once having clambered aboard, any remaining fears for its safety were instantly allayed.

"Now if only there's petrol! If only it's ready!" Her chant rang out hollowly in the tunnel and, full of hope now, she got nimbly down to her job, and before long, the welcome sound of sputtering engine and the boat's triumphal emergence from the tunnel, told her schoolfellows of her success.

They had all suffered torturing suspense till then. To Rita, the cramped position she was forced to keep made the minutes seem an age. Then, too, the rise of the water was so awesomely deliberate and inexorable. Huddled beside the unconscious man, she tried to keep her eyes off the gradual rise, though her mind had to work on the riddle of how to keep his head above water, should it wash much higher. The shelf sloped slightly towards the sea, but that gave the inner side of it an advantage of only a couple of inches at the most. Still, even those were worth an effort, Rita decided, and gingerly she tried one, pushing hard against Mr. Howard in an endeavour to edge him back the trifle that meant so much in his desperate plight.

Realization was forced on her at last, however, that she had better take a further measure while there was a chance of its being effective. Something to pillow under his head if the necessity arose of keeping water from submerging his face.

But—a pillow! What had she to use? She might have grabbed at enough seaweed to make a sort of mound, but she dared not release her hold upon the injury; even as it was, blood was still oozing from it; so she could not reach out far enough. Besides, there was the risk, if she *could* stretch out, of sliding off the ledge, made dangerously slippery by its regular washing by the tide.

Remembrance flashed upon her suddenly; they had all brought mackintoshes with them, for a storm had threatened at the start of their trip. If she could have them, there would be the pillow she required, and also a covering for the injured man. In an accident, warmth was needed to combat the effects of shock, and certainly it would be a sorry thing if her charge were soaked to the skin by the oncoming waves. Anyhow, a mackintosh covering would minimise the mischief. True, the girls had left the mackintoshes in the boat in their scurry to investigate, but one of them could be spared now to run there, Rita decided, if only she could make her demands known.

Taking advantage of an instant's lull in the wind's sound, "Coo-ee!" she called, at the loudest pitch of which her voice was capable.

The watchers above heard her; necks were craned anxiously over, their owners obviously so terrified that the sudden shout might mean an S O S that they were helpless to answer.

"What is it? Oh, what *does* she want?" Hilary cried out in an anguished tone as indistinguishable words floated up. "If only the wind and sea would keep quiet a minute, I could hear."

But as there was no chance of that, some way of getting Rita's message had to be devised and Hilary soon settled the method of it.

"My turn now!" she told her companions, grimly. "It means only four to stand the pull of the rope, but you'll manage it all right, won't you? I expect I shall be able to hear Rita if I can climb down just half way to her."

The other girls could guess what the resolution cost her. Hilary had always confessed to having no head for heights, her only advantage over them being a rather steadier nerve in emergencies. So the next few minutes saw them holding on to the rope with an even greater desperation than before, frantically trying to keep their thoughts off the ordeal through which the dangling figure below them must be passing.

Ghastly pale, she flopped helplessly among them upon her return, and for a moment or so they were afraid she had brought worse news. But at length she managed a sickly smile.

"I've done it and I can do it again now," she gasped out. "Felt sick, but I'm getting all right again. Quickly, somebody, to the boat for our macs. Rita wants them down there, and I'll manage it. This giddiness will have gone off in a minute or two. But I want to get the job over quickly before I've time to think about it, so hustle."

The girl who pelted willingly off on the errand took no account of the bumps and bruises that attended her helter-skelter journey over the rocks, and Hilary was only just keyed up for the second and longer descent when she was back again. Speedily then, with the precious bundle held together by a belt just slip-knotted round so that it could be released easily by the watcher's one free hand, Hilary slid courageously down the rope once more.

Up again a few minutes later among her anxious friends, she broke into wild weeping.

"Mr. Howard! Rita!" she sobbed. "He looks so ill, but oh, she's so brave."

With tears in their own eyes, the other girls hugged her up between them in sympathetic understanding of her strung-up state.

"And so are *you!*" one of them said, voicing a general sentiment.

CHAPTER XIII

DELIVERANCE

WITHIN the next half hour there began an exodus from land that quickly dotted the sea with craft of all kinds. The fact that nothing of the explosion had been heard at Burlton shocked the townspeople profoundly when the news, travelling like wildfire, as ill news always does, sent police, ambulance men and coastguards hurrying to give their aid and the Press reporters their attention.

It had been impossible to keep the news from Mrs. Howard. Coral's descent upon the English mistress had been in too urgent a cause to be done with caution. In fact, the mere appearance of the distraught girl in the Howards' garden, where tea had just finished, was sufficient to suggest disaster. But agitated though she was, Coral made the best of it to the delicate mother; she assured her that her son was alive and being "first aided" as well as was possible by one of the pluckiest girls who had ever lived. Coral stressed that, and feeling that it was true, she could make her reassurance convincing.

Miss Howard got only a rather confused account of the island invasion from Coral, on the way out again. Not that it mattered much, for the mistress's thoughts were mainly occupied with the accident to her brother. How badly was he hurt? Had his work and study all gone for nought? were but two of the many questions that tortured her. Rita's spectacular part in the afternoon's happening was only vaguely present in her mind until the little motor boat bobbed and swayed among others of its kind within plain sight of the rock shelf and its occupants. Then, however, as her gaze followed Coral's pointing finger, she gasped out:

"But, my *dear!* do you mean to say that Rita got down that awful precipice by that rope?"

"I do, Miss Howard," Coral responded solemnly, satisfied now that there was the right amount of awe and wonder in the lady's attitude. "With the aid of it, anyhow, and a terrible business it must have been, wondering whether she was going down to a corpse. You see, we couldn't tell whether Mr. Howard was alive or not. I found *my* bit awful enough, just getting to within earshot of her," and the girl shuddered.

Miss Howard slid a little closer and slipped a hand through Coral's arm, trying to convey by an affectionate squeeze and the look in her eyes, the feelings that she was unable to put into words just then. And it was in that fashion that the pair sat together, watching, in breathless anxiety, preparations for the rescue of the injured man and his youthful saviour.

It seemed a tedious business to the worried onlookers, but it was a delicate situation that called for the utmost care and patience. There could be no question of hauling the injured Mr. Howard up the jagged rock face, so the coastguardsmen brought all their skill into play, to take him off in a sling buoy to a waiting launch where ambulance men waited in readiness to receive him. Before even this move could be made, however, the doctor was to reach the ledge to get an idea of Mr. Howard's condition. For the medical man to land on the narrow platform, Rita had first to be taken off it. So down slid two long rope ladders and down one of them went a sturdy coastguardsman, with the intention of sending Rita up the other ladder while he mounted guard till the doctor could come down.

But there was no more climbing in store for Rita that day. She was found to be in such a cramped, exhausted and unnerved state from her ordeal, that no such hazard to her could be risked. So, as soon as a rocket had successfully carried the lifeline, she was swung away over the waves to the launch and the skilful attention of the ambulance men. Then, down the second ladder went the doctor, and at long last, anxious eyes followed the swaying progress of the sling buoy into which he and the coastguardsman, the latter helping as best he could from his ladder, had with much difficulty got the patient.

Some little time later, the doctor, accompanied by Miss Howard, emerged from the bungalow and strolled with her across the small neat lawn. The little group of girls now occupying the rustic seat, and chairs about the deserted tea-table, shot up anxiously.

"Positive human question marks!" was the

jocular beginning the doctor made. "You sit down, my dear!" this to Rita. "You'll be better off your legs for a while longer yet. Bit shaky still, eh?"

"Oh, I'm tons better, doctor," she hastily assured him, "only cross with myself for seeming such a wreck after a bit of a climb. But never mind me. It's Mr. Howard!"

He put her back into her chair and stood looking benignly down at her.

"Yes! it's Mr. Howard!" he echoed, "with just a bit of concussion and a cut wrist," adding with slow emphasis, "it wouldn't have been Mr. Howard, though, but for your 'bit of a climb,' your pluck and resource. But for you, my dear girl, there would have been no Mr. Howard alive now. He must soon have bled to death without the aid you gave him, even had the sea not claimed him. It seems a miracle that you girls were in the neighbourhood of the island as you were. I understand that you were all taking French leave, but Miss Howard is inclined to say, as I do in the circumstances, 'Thank God for that.' I'm proud to know such heroines. Shake hands, girls!"

247

They clustered in a penitent and solicitous little ring round Miss Howard after he had gone.

"Then he really thinks Mr. Howard will get on all right?"

Grace Howard beamed on her erring pupils as she replied to the searching question put by Rita.

"Really and truly! The concussion is nothing to worry about; it is comparatively slight, marvellously so, considering that he must have been blown where he was by the force of the explosion. He will have time to get over the shock a bit before his brain gets too active again."

"But what will he say when he knows his caves and all his things are wrecked? *Poor* man!" Hilary mourned.

Grace Howard shook her head and her lips were a little tremulous. "I daren't think of that just now. All I can feel at the moment is thankfulness that he is alive and likely to recover soon. If his experiments are such as to endanger his life to the extent they did to-day, I could wish he would never attempt any more. Now I must go in, girls. The nurse may want me, and there is my poor mother. But my sister is bringing you out some refreshments before you start back to school. Rita," here she took the girl's hands and held them tightly for a moment or two, "you and I can't be anything but good friends after this, can we?" and back to her troubled household she carried a lightened heart in spite of all, because of the warm-hearted smile with which Rita had answered her.

Miss Jupp, who had been informed of events by Miss Howard over the telephone, received the truants with an amount of kindliness that permanently endeared her to them. Shaken by their experiences, the seven appreciated to the full the tact she brought to bear upon this particular occasion.

"I should like to hear about everything from your own lips," she told them gently, "not in the light of a confession of your sins," here she smiled, "I simply want to know more particularly than Miss Howard could tell me by telephone all that has happened. My only remark upon the subject of breaking bounds is that I feel I shall be able to trust you not to do it in future."

CHAPTER XIV

PEACE

SENSATIONAL reports and a picture of Mr. Howard's island in the newspapers next day set the rest of the Camberside girls all agog. Back on to the pedestal of popularity on which they had first placed Rita, she was returned; in fact, all seven of the "heroines of the island" as one paper called them, were in a fair way to have their heads turned by all the fuss that was made of them.

But letters from home pleased Rita most until, on Sunday afternoon a fortnight later, lazing under a tree with Coral and Hilary near the drive gates, Rita suddenly shouted out as an open car turned into the grounds.

"Miss Howard!"

The car was pulled up quickly by that lady herself and a moment later she was hurrying to meet the three girls.

Amazedly they stared at her.

"My dears!" she cried vibrantly. "Such news! Such wonderful news! I had to hire a car to come and tell you."

"What?" they all breathed.

"First of all, my brother is doing splendidly."

"Cheers!" again they chorused.

"Remembering things!" Miss Howard added.

"Yes?" It was Rita who breathed this out questioningly, uneasiness having suddenly enveloped all three. But surely he could not be remembering anything disappointing, worrying, or Miss Howard would not look as she did.

She nodded briefly at them, and spoke in an ecstatic kind of voice.

"Remembering that—he—was—successful—on that awful day! Oh, girls! how shall I ever thank you for saving him!" and the dignified English mistress did her best to get her arms round all three of them at once.

Half an hour later, with pleased permission from Miss Jupp, they were packed into the car with her, Rita by her side, the other two in the back, making for Burlton.

"Nothing would satisfy Jack but to see and

thank you himself, Rita," Miss Howard explained; "but I hadn't the heart to carry you off and leave the other two behind. I wish I could have accommodated the rest of your party."

The young inventor had made such rapid strides towards recovery that the girls found him in a wheeled chair in the garden with his nurse.

"I'm to be allowed a paltry ten minutes for this great occasion," he said after shaking hands. "I told the doctor that *I* should explode next if he wouldn't let me see some of my rescuers. My sister told you the great news? Funny, isn't it, that the successful formula nearly did for *me!* I *thought* I was on the right track and by gad! the stuff has proved itself. What gives me cold shivers sometimes is the thought that you girls might have fallen victims to it. My sister says you were on the way to me with a thank-offering, goodness knows what for."

The story was completed then, and every bit of it came out, and so did the thankoffering.

Jack Howard fingered the fragrant contents of the delayed parcel.

"I bet these will be the nicest smokes of my life," he said softly.

Then, looking up at the girls, he added, "It's I who should make thankofferings. I owe my fortune as well as my life to the most useful spies who ever existed. Rita!" this with a special grin for the spirited leader, "you'll have to be a lady detective or a secret service agent. There's no doubt about that!"

"Oh, *isn't* there, Mr. Howard?" she retorted and shook her head at him with a vigour that set its tight curls dancing. "I'd sooner plough and sow and reap and mow for evermore. Miss Howard knows *that!*" she added with a smile that lady well understood.

Rita's return to the Priory Farm for her first holidays, was something in the nature of a triumphal occasion.

Jimmy, thrilled to the ears at his school by the newspaper reports of his sister's prowess in aid of the young inventor, managed to get home first in order to be in the family welcome accorded her. Mr. Conway, senior, full of satisfaction over the distinction gained by his favourite, a distinction much more laudable than those to be gained by book-learning, in his opinion, put up with the torture of riding with a sciatic leg to be on the spot at the farm when she arrived.

With an air vastly different from the one she had worn on her departure thirteen weeks before, she greeted the little assembly waiting for her outside the peaceful old farm house.

"Well!" she cried with a cheery grin. "I don't seem to have turned up like a *bad* penny, after all."

"Talking of money, Rita, my dear——" began her grandfather, with a smile almost as wide as her own and just as cheery.

She shook a finger at him. "I'm a very good return for any money anybody ever laid out, Grandpa," she cried challengingly.

"You are, that!" he agreed, with a great laugh over the joke that only she and he understood, as yet. "But as the secret hinted at is out," he added, "I'd like my money's worth of details, please, so come along indoors and we'll enjoy them over our lunch."

When the meal, enlivened by Rita's graphic account of all the doings, was at an end, her grandfather nodded his head benignly at her.

"Well, now! what did I say to you before you went? I *knew* you'd like school all right."

"Oh, but I *don't*, Grandpa," she flashed. "I hate *school* and I always shall, but I shall have to go on with it all the same. I couldn't possibly let Coral and all the rest sink back into the morass of dullness they were in. I *did* liven things up! So, you see," here she divided a saucy glance between her father and grandparent, "you'll never be able to do me out of dear Tommy."

Which effective "last word" sent everybody out in the highest of spirits to see her welcomed home by Tommy himself.

Priory Farm was in even more festive and jubilant mood a fortnight later.

At the nearest railway station the four young Conways positively mobbed a couple alighting from a train to be solicitously jollied along to where Mr. Conway awaited them with a big car.

"It's awfully good of you and Mrs. Conway," Mr. Howard said as he took the seat beside his host, "to have invited my sister and me for this jolly holiday."

Mr. Conway smiled warmly at the hero of the island. "You are very welcome," he replied. "Both my wife and I feel that you Howards have been instrumental in bringing us a deal of happiness, through Rita. Nothing would satisfy her but that we should get you and your sister here to recuperate after your trying experience. I understand that you're an old boy of my son's school. Jimmy hopes to take back with him some first hand information about your work. But you're here to convalesce, so don't let the youngsters make themselves a nuisance."

Mr. Howard twisted his head round to grin at the merry party behind.

"They couldn't—to *me*," he said. "A fellow who has 'hermitted' on a lonely isle as I've done for months, is only too glad of a little lively company."

"Well! you'll get it at Priory Farm," laughed its owner. "Rita will see to that!"

And Rita did so!

MADE AND PRINTED IN GREAT BRITAIN BY PURNELL AND SONS, LTD.
PAULTON (SOMERSET) AND LONDON
E4-1263